ICE

ON

FIRE

KNIGHTS OF SILENCE MC
BOOK II

AMY CECIL

ICE on FIRE- Knights of Silence MC Book II

Book cover design and layout by,
Ellie Bockert Augsburger of Creative Digital Studios.
www.CreativeDigitalStudios.com

Cover design features:

Fire flames: © Sergey Nivens / Adobe Stock

Muscular Young Man: © thodonal / Adobe Stock

Editing Services provided by,
Carl Augsburger of Creative Digital Studios.
www.CreativeDigitalStudios.com

ISBN-13: 978-1546967774 (CreateSpace-Assigned)
ISBN-10: 154696777X
BISAC: Fiction / Romance / Contemporary

DEDICATION

This book is dedicated to all the amazing individuals who are members of my street team, Amy's Amazing Street Girls. I never knew what a street team was until a few short months ago and now, I can't believe that I had gone without you all for as long as I did. Alicia Freeman and Michelle Cates, you ladies do a fantastic job managing the team. You are my superstars! I wish I could list each and every member of the team here, but that's over 400 names. Thank you for all that you do for me. You all are truly amazing!

PROLOGUE

1995 – Edinboro, Pennsylvania

Katie

"Katie, I have had about enough of Caden and his carefree attitude toward his future. If he were my ..." Tyler stopped himself. He knew better. He had obviously been about to say 'if he were my son', but he realized that those words would not fly with me. Caden isn't his son. Tyler knew that when he chose to marry me. He didn't have the right to throw it in my face after all these years.

"Ty, why can't you just accept Caden for the boy that he is? Why does he always have to measure up to some arbitrary image that you have of him? He's sixteen, Tyler. Let him be a boy before he becomes a man," I said.

"I can't do that, and you know why," he replied.

"After all these years, Ty, I am not sure that I do. Why don't you spell it out for me? 'Cause frankly, I'm sick and tired of having the same conversation with you over and over again," I replied smartly. He was irritating me as he always did whenever Caden was concerned.

"When I agreed to marry you, I made a pact with myself to ensure that Caden would not turn out like his father. Ace Corrigan is a hoodlum and an outlaw with no use for rules. I'll be damned if I allow my son to turn out like that."

"You know what, Ty? I guess you are off the hook. Because in case you forgot, Caden is not your son! He's mine!" I yelled angrily.

He made assumptions about Ace, but he'd never really known Ace. Not like I did. My words rendered him speechless and he stormed out of the room.

After Tyler left, I sat on the bed. I thought about all the mistakes I had made with my life. Sure, I had a ton of regrets. But having Caden was not one of them. My mind drifted to a happier time ...

Sixteen years earlier ...

Ace Corrigan was hot! Not just the nice to look at hot, either—no, he was the kind of hot that made your legs go weak. He was tall with a strong build. When Ace walked into a room, his presence took up the whole room. He had thick dark hair that lay just below his neck and he had the most piercing blue eyes I had ever seen. His features were chiseled with strong cheekbones. His torso was ripped and muscular and it seemed like every time I looked at him, my panties got wet.

I'd been in love with that boy since I was sixteen, or maybe even earlier than that. I'd always thought that he felt the same. He was always hanging around—not to mention the fact that he always flirted with me. But he never took it any further than just friendship, always keeping his distance from me.

It was summer break and I was home from college. I'd just finished my third year at Gettysburg College and I was so excited that I only had one more to go. Throughout the last three years away from home, Ace had always come to visit me on my breaks, usually making his first visit the day after I got home. But this time, he was late! I'd been home for several days and still hadn't seen Ace.

I'd known Ace ever since he came to Edinboro in the seventh grade. We quickly became friends, and up until recently, we'd remained that way. During our last year in high school, Ace spoke about the Knights of Silence MC often. I never knew much about the MC, but it made him happy so it never bothered me. Right before we graduated high school, Ace came to school wearing a leather vest from the Knights. The back read *Prospect*. When I asked him about it, he said that prospecting was like an initiation process for the club. It sounded like a sorority to me, but I kept that thought to myself.

By the time I finished my first year in college, Ace told me he was a full-patch member of the club. I didn't understand the difference, but was too embarrassed to ask. I guess if I really thought about it, I figured being a prospect was a temporary thing to see if you could cut it. Maybe it was also to see if they liked you and you liked them kinda thing? Becoming a full-patch member must have meant they liked you and you were in the club for life. Or something like that. Anyway, Ace had been in the club for a few years now and I had seen him change from a boy into a man much quicker than I would have wanted. I thought about our high school days and he just seemed to grow up a lot faster than I did. I didn't mind the changes one bit—however, I'd noticed that each time I saw him he seemed to drift further away from me. *Maybe that is why he hasn't come to visit this time. Perhaps he doesn't have time for me anymore*, I thought sadly.

I'd been home for a full week now and still hadn't heard a word from Ace. I'd tried to call and text, but he didn't respond. Feeling sorry for myself and not being able to hear another question from Mom or Dad about why I was so down, I decided to just hang out on the front porch. After sitting there for almost an hour, I heard it. It was the sound I had longed to hear: the roar of a motorcycle. This wasn't just any motorcycle, either—no, this iron horse was a Harley. Ace had taught me the difference between the sound of a Harley and other motorcycles. Harleys have a distinct sound and I could pick one out anywhere, anytime. I may not have known a lot about motorcycle clubs and their protocols, but I sure as hell knew about motorcycles, thanks to Ace. I loved them, and always loved it when Ace would take me for a ride on his bike.

The sound of the bike got closer and I sat on the swing, anxiously hoping it was Ace. The motorcycle turned the corner and I immediately recognized his broad build coming toward me. His

MC cut identified him as a member of the club, but the helmet he wore was his and his alone. It was a black full helmet with the most menacing green dragon coiled around it. It was gorgeous and I could not have been happier. Ace had finally come to see me.

He pulled up in front of the house, turned the motor off, and then took off his helmet. Still sitting on his bike, looking like a Harley Davidson God, he turned to me and smiled. His piercing blue eyes sparkled in the sunlight and his jet-black hair blew in the wind. And that was it. That was all it took for every bone in my body to turn to mush. I could feel my legs become weightless and was thankful that I was still sitting down. This man was gorgeous and I fell in love with him all over again—not that I'd ever stopped, but he definitely had a way about him that would make any woman fall hard for him. He slowly dismounted his bike and his full 6'5" frame came into view. His chest was broad, but his body narrowed at the waist, and all I could think about as I watched him saunter up my walk was what it would feel like to have him in my bed. Not that I'd had any man in my bed ... but truth be told, I never thought about it with other guys, just Ace. I knew he was the only man I would ever want.

When he got to the porch he finally spoke. "Hey, Katie Bug!"

Oh God, I thought to myself, *I can feel the moisture pooling between my legs. How can three words from him do this to me?* Nonchalantly as I could, I replied, "Hey there! It's about time you came by."

"I'm late, I know. Been out of town on a run, just got back this morning. Couldn't be helped, babe."

"No worries," I replied. "It's good to see you."

He got up to the porch, approached me, and then just stood there. His body towered over mine. He smelled so darn good. I didn't want to be too obvious by sniffing at him, so I held back the urge to do so.

"Don't you got a hug for me?" he asked, holding out his arms and inviting me in.

He didn't need to coax me; my body naturally fell into his arms. His hugs were strong, protective, and warm. Nothing made

4

me feel better or safer than being in his arms. "It's good to see you too, Katie Bug! I've missed your face," he said.

I loved it when he called me Katie Bug. I loved it when he said he missed my face. I loved everything about this man and one day, I was going to tell him.

After the hug, we sat down on the porch and talked about all that had happened over the last couple of months. Time always flew by when Ace and I were together, and after glancing down at my watch I soon realized that he'd been at the house for a couple of hours and we had spent the entire time sitting on the front porch, talking and laughing. *Why doesn't he see the connection we have? I know it's not my imagination. There is chemistry between the two of us that I just can't explain. But other than a welcome hug and an occasional light kiss on the cheek, he keeps his distance. Why?*

Just then, Tyler Jackson pulled up in his BMW i8. He thought he was hot shit in that car, but very few knew it was his daddy's car. I knew it, but he still had to put on airs around others, especially those he felt were inferior to him. Our parents had always anticipated that Tyler and I would get married when we both graduated from college. We'd been friends for a long time and he'd been trying to get in my pants since I was seventeen, but I wasn't going to have it. I never liked Tyler that way. Besides, I was saving myself for the man that I was actually going to marry. That man would not be Tyler. I was certain that I would marry Ace. My family may not have liked my choice, but it was just that. My choice.

When Ace saw Tyler pull up, he looked over at me and got up from the chair he was sitting in. He said sadly, "I better go, Katie Bug. Talk to you later?"

"You know, you don't have to leave, Ace. This is my house, and you are welcome here anytime. I love your company and the time that we spend together. It's the one thing I look forward to about coming home. It makes me sad that we never see each other anymore. I would like you to stay."

"I know, sweetie, but it is better that I go and keep the peace. Talk to you later, doll face." He looked at me sadly, kissed me on the cheek, and then turned to leave. He didn't comment on us spending time together, nor did he acknowledge anything about liking our time together too. He never said anything about seeing me again this summer. Everything was left up in the air, as always.

"I will never understand why you associate yourself with those people," Tyler said as he walked up the sidewalk to my house, just as Ace was getting on his bike to leave. Ace looked over to me reluctantly. I was so embarrassed, as I was sure he'd heard Tyler. Ace fired up his bike and nodded to me as he drove off. I made it a point to intentionally wait for the roar of Ace's bike to fade in the distance before I responded to Tyler's comment. He just stood there looking annoyed with me as he waited for a response.

Irritated, I turned toward Tyler and said, "I talk to *those people* because I like them, and they are very nice—especially Ace. I've known Ace since the seventh grade, Tyler, and you know he's always been a dear friend to me. Maybe if you removed that stick from your butt and got to know him you might be surprised."

He just shook his head.

Giggling, I added, "What are you afraid of, Tyler? Are you worried that you might actually *like* him?"

Angrily, he responded, "Katie, I will never like them or that Ace character. They are a bunch of hoodlums, and I don't like you associating with them."

Oh no, he doesn't get to do that. If he wants to be my friend, he doesn't get any say on who is or who isn't my friend. I thought to myself. Out loud, I said "Look, Ty, it doesn't work that way. If you want us to continue being friends, then you need to remember that I will be friends with whomever I want."

"But Katie, they ..."

I immediately interrupted him. "Stop! This is not up for discussion. Understood?"

Angrily, he responded, "Fine! If you want to associate with Ace and his merry band of bikers, you go ahead and do that. I'm going places, and I will not allow your shady acquaintances to hinder me."

"Hinder you? Are you for real? We're just friends, Tyler. How could I hinder you?" I asked, totally floored by his comment.

"Well ... well ... I just might want us to be more than friends. What do you think about that?" he said nervously.

6

I was speechless. That was the last thing I'd expected him to say. I liked Tyler. Well, sometimes. Right then, I didn't like him at all. But even when I did like him, I never thought of him that way. I knew our parents thought differently, but … no. Absolutely not. I wanted passion and adventure in my life, and Tyler wasn't the guy to give it to me. The only man that would give me what I wanted was Ace. He may have been rough and tough on the outside, but to me, he had always been sweet, charming, and so damn sexy. I knew that one day soon he was going to realize that we were meant to be together.

I knew I had to give Tyler a response. *What do I say to him? It's probably not the best idea to tell him that I think he is boring. And it would be even worse to mention Ace in this conversation. That would be funny, though—I bet I could actually make steam come from his ears. But it wouldn't be nice and wouldn't make me any better than he is being right now.* Trying to be as tactful as I could, I said, "Tyler, that is very sweet, but right now I think it best that you and I just remain friends." *There, that wasn't so bad. Was it?*

Tyler didn't look too happy with my response … perhaps even a little embarrassed. He was quiet for a moment and I could see him getting back his composure. He then nodded and said, "Your mind will change, I'm sure of it. I'm not giving up hope, Katie. Someday, you and I will be married. We both come from good, upstanding families; it's the only thing that makes sense to me." He paused for a moment and then added, "Well, I better go. I guess I will see you tomorrow."

I didn't know what else to say, so I just responded with, "Ok Ty, see you later."

One month later …

I had a couple of weeks left before I had to go back to school and I'd only seen Ace twice. I tried calling him a couple of times but he never answered. When I would send texts, his response was always the same:

> In the middle of something, can't talk now.

I had really thought that this was the summer that I would finally get my man. But to my complete disappointment, another summer break had come and gone and Ace and I had gotten nowhere.

I decided to send him one last text:

> I'm heading back to school in a couple of weeks. Would love to see you before I leave.

I pushed send and waited. And waited. And waited. A week went by and I had pretty much given up on Ace. I spent the last few days staring out the front window of the house, hoping that he would come by. I was depressed and moping. I knew it was driving Mom and Dad crazy, but I couldn't talk to them about it. They would just tell me to spend more time with Tyler, and that was the last thing I felt like doing.

After a couple of weeks of moping around the house, I finally decided that it was time to forget about Ace and move on. I was not going to get to see him before I left for school and I feared that I would never see him again.

A few hours later, Mom and I were busy in the kitchen when I heard the most wonderful sound: the rumble of Ace's Harley as it pulled into our driveway. As he sat on his bike taking off his helmet, I watched him closely through the kitchen window. *Damn, he's hot.* He was wearing his cut, sporting the Knights of Silence MC colors. He was not what you would expect to see in my neighborhood, but his leather, tattoos, and scruffier look definitely made him sexier than any of the boys that lived around me. Especially Tyler. He hung his helmet on his handlebars and grinned up at the window. He knew I was watching him because he knew exactly where I was.

I said, "Mom, Ace is here. I'll be right back."

"Katie, you need to tell that boy that you are not interested in him," she said.

"No Mom, I don't. That would be lying," I replied.

"Katie, since when have you been interested in Ace?" Mom asked.

I shook my head in disbelief. Was she really that thick? "How about for as long as I have known him?" I responded.

"But Katie, he's a hoodlum. He's a biker. He's bad news, sweetheart, and he is only going to break your heart," she said pleadingly, as if she thought her words were going to miraculously change my mind.

"You know what Mom, just drop it. You will never understand and I really want to talk to Ace," I said as I headed out of the kitchen and to the door. She called after me, but I just didn't want to continue the conversation with her. I knew it was rude, but I was over eighteen and I'd had enough.

When I got outside, I strolled casually down the driveway toward Ace and his bike. He was freakin' gorgeous! "Hey, beautiful!" he said. "You look fantastic!" I was wearing a short, full, summer skirt and a t-shirt—nothing fancy, but definitely not the type of outfits he was used to seeing on the women who hung around his club.

He made me smile immediately, but then I remembered I was mad at him. "Don't you go and try to butter me up, Ace Corrigan! I'm mad at you!" I paused, and then asked, "Where have you been all summer?"

"I've been busy, Katie Bug. Club stuff. You know how it is," he replied. I didn't know how it was. He would never tell me. He then added, "So, let's start over. Hey, beautiful! You look fantastic!"

Damn him. He knew I couldn't stay mad at him for long. I caved and said teasingly, "Thanks, Dragon Slayer. You don't look so bad yourself."

"Why do you call me that?" he asked.

"You mean you don't know?" I said coyly.

"You call me that all the time, but you have never told me why. Tell me," he said.

"Well, if you must know, you make all the bad things go away. All my fears, all the things that frighten me ... you slay them. You are my dragon slayer, Ace. You always have been. You always will be."

"Katie Bug, I can't be all that for you, darl'n. I never know where I'll be from one day to another. This is no life for you, and I don't want this life for you. You deserve so much better than an outlaw biker like me."

"Then why do you keep coming to see me?" I asked. "This summer was the perfect opportunity for you to cut your ties with me. I thought you had."

He shook his head, seeming disgusted with himself. "Because I can't stay away. You are like a breath of fresh air in the very dark world that I live in. All it took was your text a week ago to let me know that you were leaving. I knew I couldn't let you leave without saying goodbye."

I looked at him smugly. "See, you need me!"

Changing the subject, he said, "Why don't you go change and we can go for a ride."

I shook my head. "No, I can go like this!"

"No, your skirt thingy will be flying up all over the place and everyone will be able to see," he said, not pleased by my suggestion.

"Look Ace, if I go back in the house, I doubt that my mom will just let me leave with you without an argument. If I promise to hold my skirt down, can we please just go? Please?" I said.

"You are one crazy woman, Katie Bug." He shook his head again. "Hop on!"

I jumped on his bike and he backed out of the driveway. I knew Mom would be angry that I left, but I wouldn't be gone long. When we got to the bottom of the driveway, Ace revved his Harley and we were off. God, I loved riding on the back of his bike—being so close to him, my body warm and hot up against him. I thought I had died and gone to heaven.

He drove us to Liana's Lake Park. It was dusk and the sun was setting on the lake. It was beautiful. When he brought the bike to a stop, I hopped off. It was now or never, and I had to make my move. Before he had a chance to get off the bike himself, I swung my leg over his bike and straddled the tank. My back was facing the handlebars. I inched myself up closer to him, and he made a deep groan as our chests touched. Without hesitation his hand slid up under my skirt and he ran his fingers along my thighs. He reached my core and just hovered there as he leaned in and kissed me. It was our first kiss. It was a deep, passionate kiss, and I didn't want it to end. I had been kissed before, but not like that. It was amazing.

We finally broke apart just long enough to breathe, and then he kissed me again. The passion that we both had been holding in all those years finally erupted into flames and suddenly we couldn't get enough of each other. His hand reached underneath my panties and he began to stroke me. I felt like I was about to explode; the pleasure was unbearable. I was holding on to him, my arms encircled around his neck. His left hand was working me over while his right hand was holding me so tight against him I couldn't move. I wanted him. Hell, I'd always wanted him, but just then it was more urgent than usual.

He released his right hand and reached down to undo his jeans. After he freed his cock, I was amazed at the size of it and suddenly felt very wet. He groaned again as he hiked my body up on top of him. "Ride me, baby," he said, and it was my undoing. He slid my underwear to the side as I worked to impale myself on him. He was huge, and suddenly I was overcome with the fear of his size. But I couldn't stop, not even if I wanted to. I slowly pushed myself down on him. When he broke through my barrier, the pain was excruciating. I tensed. "Katie?" he asked, concerned. "What's wrong, Katie Bug?" I looked up into his eyes tearfully and I saw the realization come across his face. "Fuck, Katie, you're a virgin!" I nodded. "It shouldn't be this way, babe. It should be special. Not frantic sex on my bike." He tried to break free, but I stopped him.

The last thing I wanted was for him to stop. My friends had told me that sex for the first time would hurt, but if I just waited for my body to adjust to him, it wouldn't be so bad. "Ace, please don't stop. I want this! Please!" I knew I sounded like a child, but I had dreamed about being with him for so long and feared that I would never get this chance again. I couldn't let him stop now, no matter how bad it hurt. "Just let me get used to you for a minute. I'll be fine," I said pathetically.

"Katie, I can't. I can't promise you anything after this," he said.

"Please," I begged. "I don't care about promises, I just want you."

"Katie, you're killing me. Do you have any idea how hard it is to say no to you, even if I know it's the right thing to do?"

"Well, if it is so hard for you, then why are we having this conversation?" I asked coyly.

"Fuck it, I'm a selfish bastard. Always have been, always will be," he said as he grabbed my hips and slowly moved me on him. There was still some discomfort, but my body was adjusting to his and as the discomfort began to subside, the feeling of him filling me was overwhelming. I began to relax. He must have known it was feeling better because he began moving me in a way that worked us both into a frenzy. Filling me completely, he called out my name as he found his release. As he was pumping his seed into me he reached down and began to massage my clit. It didn't take long to find that I was reaching an orgasm too.

"Fuck, Katie Bug. That was amazing," he said.

"Thank you for not stopping. I've wanted this for so long." A long silence stretched between us. The moment was scaring me, and I just had to ask, "Ace. Does this mean that I'm your old lady now?" *Oh shit, I can't believe I just said that.*

He looked directly into my eyes and I could see the love he had for me. He moved a hair away from my face and just looked at me for what seemed like forever. Then he spoke. "Katie, I love you. I've always loved you. But you being my old lady is not in the cards for us. You deserve a better life than what I can offer you, babe. I've told you this numerous times."

"I know, but a life with you is the only life I want. Don't you think I should decide what is best for me or what I deserve?" I asked.

"Not this time, babe. You think hooking up with a biker is an idealistic fairytale life. It's not. We kill and we get killed. It's not pretty, and I will not subject you to that kind of life. I don't care how much you plead with me, it's not going to happen. Besides, you will be much better off with Tyler what's-his-name."

"I don't want him! I want you!" I yelled.

"Katie, I'm not gonna change my mind. You have always known this. I have made this perfectly clear to you for a while now. I've kept my distance on purpose, Katie. I never wanted to give you false hope that there could be anything more between us," he replied.

"So you basically just stole my virginity and now you are saying goodbye?" I said angrily. I didn't care that there would be danger. At least I could face that danger with him at my side. Despite my anger, I knew this had not been about just getting into my pants or fucking the virgin. I knew Ace too well for that. It was obvious how he felt about me and I knew without a doubt he loved me.

"Katie, it's not like that, and you know it. I told you that I couldn't make any promises to you, that I couldn't offer you anything beyond this. You agreed."

"I did not!" I yelled.

"You did and you know it. If my life was different ... hell, we would already be married. We'd have a couple of kids and the white picket fence. But my life is not different. My life requires me to have no connections to anything that I love. I can't afford to love. They will come after what I love most, and I will not put you in that position. I love you too much."

"What do you mean, 'they'?" I asked.

"My enemies, the club's enemies. They are everywhere, baby, and I will not put you smack-dab in the center of all the chaos. I will not do it!"

"Take me home, Ace," I demanded. I didn't want to hear any more. He was telling me goodbye when I'd thought our life was just starting.

Ace drove me home. It was dark as we pulled into the driveway. As I got off his bike, I turned to him and said, "I love you."

He reached over and tugged on my arm, pulling me tight to his body. His hand reached up into my hair and he eased my head forward. His lips were hovering next to my ear. "Forgive me, my beautiful Katie Bug. I will always love you more," he whispered in my ear, sending chills all through my body. He released me, pushed his bike back down the drive, and left.

As he pulled away, I muttered to myself, "Holy shit! We didn't use any protection."

Three months later ...

My life was over. It was my wedding day. You would think I would have been a nervous, overly happy bride. But no, I wasn't that bride. This was not the wedding I wanted. It was not the wedding of my dreams, and the groom definitely was not the man I wanted to marry. I knew I would always remember my wedding with sadness and fear for the life I was being forced to live. I was marrying a man I would never love. I appreciated what Tyler was doing for me, but I knew I would never love him. Not like I loved Ace. But Ace didn't want his child or me. He'd made that perfectly clear.

Present day
Caden

"Message received. You got me," I said.

Mark's satanic laugh echoed through the phone. He'd been clear. I only had two options: I either had to allow his vengeance to destroy everything that I loved—Emma, Ari, and my club—or allow him to destroy me. The choice was easy. Emma would survive. I had put enough money away that Ari would want for nothing in the event that something would happen to me. It was more than her father ever did for her. My club would also survive and most likely flourish without me. Hawk would take over as President. The club and Edinboro would find peace again. It was an easy choice. It was time to face my half-brother.

His instructions were clear. I was to meet him in Wattsburg. That was roughly 30 minutes from the shattered clubhouse that lay before me. I turned to Honey, who was devastated by what just happened, and said, "Call Hawk. Tell him what has happened here and that I've found Emma. He'll know what to do." She looked at me confused and I added, "I have to go." I turned to leave.

"Ice, wait," she called after me. I turned and she asked, tears welling up in her eyes, "Where are you going?" Somehow, I sensed that she knew exactly what I was about to do. I didn't know how, she but she'd always had a sixth sense when any members of the club were about to head into danger. I could tell by the look in her eyes that she believed that this was the last time she was gonna see me.

I needed her to help Hawk and the boys heal the club. She couldn't break down on me now. I walked over to her, kissed her on the forehead, and said as calmly as I could, "Now don't you go worrying your pretty little head, darl'n, I'll be back."

CHAPTER 1

Emma

"Caden will come for me ..."

Time ticked away so slowly. I couldn't tell if it was night or day. I couldn't tell how long I had laid here on this filthy bed, naked and bound.

"Caden will come for me ..."

But I was wrong. My last thought before I lost consciousness again was that nobody had come for me.

I awoke to rapid and frantic talking outside my door. *Is Caden here? He did come for me, just like I knew he would!* As I strained to listen to what was being said, I realized the only voice I could hear was Mark's. He sounded frantic, and as his words faded in and out, I realized that he was pacing up and down outside the door. *What is going on? Could Caden be here and he just hasn't said anything? Or is Mark really out there talking to himself?* I couldn't make out what Mark was saying at first, but then his words progressively got louder.

"What the fuck are you gonna do, Mark?"

"Shut up! Shut up! I've got this!"

"No you don't, you don't have shit!"

"Fuck you! Shut up! You don't know what the hell you're talking about!"

"If I don't know what I'm talking about, then tell me—what are you gonna do? You've got him in the basement and her in that room. You gonna do what you promised? You need to follow through with your promise to him!"

"NO! I DON'T!! I can take them both down now. Him for stealing from me what was rightfully mine and her for being a royal pain in the ass that I have had to deal with for the past several years. She was only a means to an end, you knew that."

"Of course I did, but did you?"

"What the fuck! You are fucking with my head! Get out!"

"Mark, I will never leave you, you know that."

"GET OUT! GET OUT! GET THE FUCK OUT OF MY HEAD!"

The door burst open and a minimal amount of light crept through the opening. Mark stormed into the room and stared at me. He was creeping me out more than he had when he was in this room before. Then, he had been calm, calculated, and eerie. Now, he appeared unhinged, frantic, and nervous. He was still staring down at me wide-eyed, but then he turned to his right and whispered, "So, asshole, what are you gonna do?"

He then turned to the left and said a little louder, "I'm gonna do what I planned to do and there is no way in hell you are going to stop me."

He turned back to his right and whispered again, "Think about this, Mark. You fuck this up and you can kiss your career goodbye. Do you really believe the Knights will welcome you into their club after this? Do you really think you have anywhere to go, even now? You're done. It's all over."

He turned back to his left and yelled, "I will do what I fucking damn well please. Get out!" He then turned back toward me and yelled, "Get out!" I was so confused by what I'd just witnessed that I was unsure whether or not he was talking to me. He threw my clothes at me and ordered, "Get dressed!" He walked over to me undid the ties that bound me and ordered again, "Get dressed! Get out!"

Not wanting to argue with him, I did as I was told. My arms and legs were stiff and felt like jelly at the same time. I was having trouble getting myself to stand steady constantly needing to hold on to something, which made putting my clothes on difficult. Once I was able to balance myself and stand on my own two feet I began to get dressed, as he demanded. As I was buttoning my jeans, my curiosity about what was going on was killing me and I just had to ask, "Mark, what's happened?"

He gave me no response. He wouldn't even look at me.

I prodded, saying, "Why are you letting me go? Where's Caden? Is Caden here?"

Again, he gave me no response, but smirked at the mention of Caden. I was confused. Where was Cade, or any of the other Knights? Were they here? Would I find them outside? I had no idea, but at this point, I figured that I was not going to get any answers from Mark and the best thing to do was to get my butt out of this hell hole while I had the chance. I finished getting dressed and rushed over to the door.

Finally, he looked at me and yelled, "GET OUT!"

I had no idea where I was or how I was going to get back home. I walked out of the room and entered a dark hallway. Not knowing how to get out of the house that I was in, I looked to him for some form of direction.

He said, "Down the hall and then take the first right. Now GO!" I followed his instructions and as I was walking down the hall I remember him saying something to himself about having *him* downstairs. In the hopes that it was Cade, I yelled, "Caden! Caden, he's letting me go!"

He quickly came up behind me and pushed me forward. "Not another word! Now get the fuck out before I change my mind!"

I ran outside the door and found myself alone. Neither Caden nor the Knights were outside to rescue me. Mark did not follow me; he just slammed the door behind me.

Now what do I do? I found myself in an area that I was not familiar with. I turned back toward the building that I'd been held captive in and was surprised to see that it was a quaint little cottage. It was well-kept, with a perfectly manicured lawn and flowers adorning the front walk. Two rocking chairs were on the front porch. Nobody would ever begin to imagine the horrors that lie within.

My cell phone was in the back pocket of my jeans, but the battery was dead. I didn't know Cade's number, but it was programmed into that phone. It was the only number programmed into that phone. Rebel had taken my personal cell phone when we headed up to the safe house and all I was left with was this burner. I didn't have any form of transportation, so I began to walk. I had no idea where I was going, but I hoped I would be able to find a place with a phone. After walking for several miles, I came to a gas station. *Thank God.* I was exhausted, and that gas station was the first ray of hope I'd had since Mark let me go.

I approached the clerk and asked, "Do you have a phone I could use?"

The clerk looked at me curiously. I must have looked awful; I was sure that my face was bruised and swollen from the blows Mark had given me. She did not ask any questions but just handed over her personal cell phone.

Holding her phone in my hands, I realized I had no idea who to call. I just stood there for several seconds in a daze. Then I turned back to her and asked, "Do you have a phone number for a cab company?" She went in the back and came out with a phone book and handed it to me. "Thank you."

I found a cab company and called. When they answered, I asked if I could get a cab and their response was, "Where are we picking you up, ma'am?"

I had no idea where I was. I looked back up to the clerk and asked, "Excuse me, but can you tell me where I am?"

Finally, the clerk spoke. She said, "You're in Wattsburg." She grabbed a piece of paper on the side of the register and began writing. She handed it to me and I repeated the address that she had written down to the man on the phone. He told me he would be there in twenty minutes. I thanked him and handed the clerk her phone back, thanking her as well.

I paced around the store while waiting for my ride. I was starving and thirsty, but I had no money. After a few minutes I began getting antsy. The clerk watched me curiously. After about ten minutes, she asked, "Hun, are you ok?"

I looked over at her and began to cry. She came out from behind the counter and gave me a hug. She didn't know me from

Adam, but her concern was genuine. "I'm ok. I just need to get home."

"Do you want me to call the police?"

My response was too immediate, but I could not help it. "No!" I could not get the police involved until I knew what had happened to Cade and the Knights. I had to put the pieces of the puzzle together before I brought in an outside party that I was not sure that I could trust. Fortunately, my cab soon pulled up. As I hurried out of the store, I realized I had no money to pay for the cab. Just then, the clerk came running out of the store. As I was about to explain to the driver about my money situation, she came up to me and handed me a $50 bill. I looked at her, shocked by her generosity.

"Hopefully, this will get you home," she said. When I protested, she insisted. "You look like you could use some kindness. Just promise me something: get some help." She smiled at me as her eyes began to tear up. It occurred to me just then that she thought I had been raped. Luckily for me, that was not the case. I thanked her and promised that I would find her to pay her back. I turned to get in the cab.

I had the driver take me to the Knights' clubhouse, only to find the place burnt to the ground. *Oh my God. What has happened?* I thought to myself. *Is everyone dead?*

Shocked and discouraged by what I'd just seen and knowing of no other places where I could find Caden, I asked the driver to take me back to my apartment. When I got there I noticed a box sitting outside my apartment door. Suddenly I realized that I didn't have a key to get into my apartment. *Will Brianne be home?* I thought. *Brianne! What has happened to her?* I had totally forgotten about her and her part in all of this. *Is she ok? Is Caden? Where is everyone?*

I tried the door, hoping that she was home safe. It was locked. I knocked, but there was no answer. I went back to the lobby where the management office was located, hoping they would be able to let me into my apartment. Luckily the girl working that day knew me and unlocked my apartment. I carried the box in and reluctantly opened it. Inside were the personal items that I'd had with me at the safe house, along with my purse and keys. *Did they return my car?* I hadn't noticed it in the parking lot, but after looking out the window, I saw it parked just outside my window.

There wasn't a note, but I assumed that Caden or someone from the Knights had brought the package over. After going through the box, I walked straight to my bedroom, sat on the bed, and cried. I was free, but I had never been more frightened than I was at that moment. The memories of the last twenty-four hours flooded back into my mind. I kept asking myself, *where is Cade? Where is Brianne? Why hasn't Caden come for me? What happened to the Knights?* Then the most horrifying thought entered my mind: *Could they all be dead?*

I knew the memories of the last twenty-four hours would haunt me for the rest of my life. Being kidnapped by Mark was the worst experience of my life. But I'd survived. I hoped that one day I would understand why Mark did what he did, what his connection to Cade was, and why he suddenly let me go.

Nobody had come for me and I had no idea where any of the club members were. After I had charged my cell phone's battery on the burner, I tried calling Cade, but my calls always went to voicemail. My texts were left unanswered. I felt as if I had I left the world I had known and been transported to a world of total uncertainty, all in a matter of 24 hours. I was utterly alone and very tired. *Perhaps if I just lie down for a bit, things will look brighter when I wake up,* I thought to myself.

When I woke the next morning, for a brief moment, I had forgotten all that had transpired over the last couple of days. And then, like a flood, every horrible memory came back. As I began to cry for everything that was uncertain and most likely lost to me, I started to get angry. I was not a victim. I would not allow Mark to win and take the people that I loved most in this world away from me.

I got myself out of bed and began to start my day. I needed a plan. First, I was going to go back to the clubhouse and see if I could find anyone that might know something. After that, I had no idea … but it was a start. I was a fighter, and I would not let the events of my past dictate my future.

CHAPTER 2

Caden

"Caden! Caden, he's letting me go!" I heard Emma screaming from upstairs. Was he really going to honor his agreement and let her go? After watching him with her last night, I had my doubts. He could be staging this for my benefit. The son of a bitch was so twisted, I didn't know what to think. The only thing I knew was that I had to act and act fast.

Last night he had my girl naked and tied to a bed with a camera on her. He touched her in places he had no business touching her. He almost raped her, and he made me watch all of it. *That fucker! Whether he has let her go or not, I need to get myself free and give him what I promised—exactly what he deserves.*

When Mark tied my restraints last night, I knew exactly what I was doing. I sat there obediently, allowing him to think that I had given in to him wholeheartedly. I really don't think he believed I would fight back. Not while he held Emma captive. But my brother didn't know me as well as he thought. I sat there and let him tie my restraints, but I kept my elbows locked into my sides. By doing this I'd given Mark a false sense of space between my wrists. So he was not aware that I had slack in my wrists and could basically free myself anytime.

Last night, while watching him with Emma, I was ready to. But I couldn't go up there half-cocked, not knowing exactly what I was walking into. I had no idea if he was alone, or if there were ten

Satans protecting him. But if he had raped her, I don't think I would have had any common sense in my brain and I am sure I would have reacted immediately. Thank fuck he didn't!

Now, if what I was perceiving was true, Emma was out of this house. But whether that was true or not, it was the perfect opportunity to act. I knew it would be the only opportunity I'd have to save us both. I freed my hands and walked over to a table covered with several knives and other metal objects—objects I had never seen before and was damn sure I was not going to find out what they were used for. I grabbed a claw hammer and a carving knife from the table. They would work perfectly for what I had in mind for this fucker.

I walked over to the bottom of the steps, pushed myself into the dark corner against the wall, and waited. I knew that Mark would definitely come down, especially if Emma were truly gone from this place. I must have waited for roughly fifteen minutes when I heard the door upstairs open. Mark came rushing down the steps, talking. I was expecting to see someone come behind him, but nobody followed.

"I should not have let her go," he said.

"But it was the right thing to do."

"Fuck you! You wouldn't know the right thing to do if it hit you smack in the face!"

I thought, *Holy shit! He has lost his mind even more than I thought.*

When he got to the bottom of the steps he said, "Fuck!" as I bludgeoned him on the side of the head with the side of the claw hammer. He stumbled and fell to the floor.

Fucker! That will teach you to mess with my girl!

Surprisingly, he tried to get up, but he couldn't. It didn't help matters much that in addition to the terrible pain he must have been feeling from the blow to the head, I was holding him down with my foot pressed firmly to his throat. "You messed with the wrong guy, *brother!*" I said. I grabbed him and dragged him over to the table. I needed to secure him. I looked over on the table and found rope and duct tape. That would do. This fucker was not going anywhere.

After I got him bound, I looked around the basement. Over on the far side I saw a hook screwed into one of the rafters. It was perfect! I dragged his ass over to the hook, grabbed the back of his shirt, and attached him to the hook so that his feet barely touched the floor. He was upright and completely at my mercy. I was surprised that he was still alive after that blow to the head. Was he coherent? No. But the fucker was still breathing. That wouldn't last long.

I stare at him for the longest time while he hung in his own basement. There was no way in hell this man could be my brother. But then I realized that there was a part of me that could be just as psychotic as he was. Just look at what I'd done to Ace's killers. Hell, look at what I was doing to Mark. I knew I could be cold-blooded and ruthless, but was I like him?

No! No fucking way! I remembered everything that he had put us through over the last couple of weeks. I remembered how my club had almost went up in smoke from his explosion. I remembered his threats, and I knew I would never forget what he'd done to Emma. I remembered his hands on her and her tears. I'd made a promise to myself that I would never go there again, but a man can only take so much. I was done being Mr. Nice Guy. I had had enough!

I took the carving knife and cut off his shirt. I was glad he was still breathing. I was hoping that he would feel what I was about to do to him. Ever so slowly I began to work. He screamed when I first started, but I think I lost him not long after the work began.

I was an artist with the knife and created a masterpiece on his body. I cut the flesh away from his chest, creating flames where the flesh was removed. They were large and there was blood everywhere, but I didn't care. The cut pieces of flesh were laid out on the table in the same design that was now on Mark's chest. Happy with my latest work of art, I stepped back to admire my handiwork. It was my signature, and was exactly what I'd done to the fucker who killed Ace. I was pleased. Mark Grayson was dead.

His battered body hung from the basement ceiling, lifeless. It was time for me to leave. I needed to make sure that Emma got out safe. I needed to get back to my club.

No, wait. I had to take a minute and think this one through. *Fuck, I can't do that. Mark had strong ties to the Satans. They could be here now, outside, or perhaps watching the house. When they find out what I have done, they will retaliate ... and they will know it was me who did it. Especially after the last time I tangled with the Satans. But they won't come after me, no, they'll come after what I loved most—Emma, Ari, and my club. I can't let that happen.*

I took a couple of deep breaths and got my thoughts together. The last thing I needed to do was to move forward unprepared. *I have to be sensible and I have to be sure that there'll be no retaliation. Hell, if I can actually get myself in a situation where I can sit down and talk with the Satans, perhaps we can establish a peace between the two clubs. This bloody rivalry has gone on long enough. But before I can do that, the Satans need to think that I am dead. Members of the Knights have to believe it, too. This will buy me time to get things in order. It will ensure that for the time being, everyone remains whole. For now, it is the only way.*

I knew that once Hawk found Grayson he'd know without any doubt that I was still alive. He'd also know me well enough to know that I had a reason for staying away. *I should call Hawk and tell him what's going on. Wait, no, that won't work.* Hawk would be the logical one to call, but not this time. His first reaction had to be a reaction to my death, and I really didn't believe he was a good actor. As VP, he would take my place as President. The Satans would be watching him. I couldn't have him giving anything away. Instead, I decided to call Rebel. Rebel was the cool and calm brother. He never cracks and shows very little emotion. He'd be able to cover better than any other club member until the time is right. When the time comes, he could inform Hawk of my plans. Once I'd gotten that all figured out, my biggest worry was what the club would do with Grayson's body. They needed to give me time before the Satans found out he was dead.

I cautiously went upstairs. I couldn't risk running into anyone who might be there as an accomplice or protection for Mark. The house was empty. I walked around and found the room where that asshole held Emma. I stared at the bed where she had been bound, naked and scared. The bile began to rise from my stomach and settle into my throat. I couldn't look any more and had to get the fuck out of that house. *That fucker is so lucky he's dead!* Wasting no more time thinking about things I couldn't change, I checked outside. It looked like everything was clear. I went out the back door and headed for the garage where Grayson had me park my bike when I arrived yesterday. Thank fuck the keys were still in the ignition. I did another look around and from what I could tell I was alone. I started up my bike and took off.

When I got away from the house from hell, I immediately found a place in Wattsburg to store my bike. I didn't need to be seen riding around on my Fat Boy. Next to the storage place was a used car lot. I found a car and paid cash for it. I really hated driving in a cage, but what choice did I have? I stored my cut and any identification to the Knights with my bike. I found a cheap hotel on the outskirts of town and paid cash for a three-month stay. If the situation took longer to resolve than that, I'd just extend my stay. The place was a dump and I didn't expect people to be knocking down their door for rooms anytime soon. For the time being, I was just a guy with no connections to anyone or anything. It was crucial that, for now, I remain under the radar.

I'd spent the last few hours watching the club muddle through what was left of our clubhouse. I was off to the side of where the bikes were parked, not far from Hawk and Ryder. I had overheard Hawk tell Ryder that he had already made arrangements for a new clubhouse. He told him that he had found an abandoned warehouse out on highway 99, just a few miles outside of town. I knew the place and it was a good choice. It would be better than what we'd had—after a few modifications, of course. We wouldn't have to do too much, but we would have to up fit the space to account for the separate rooms and the bar, and of course we would have to get all-new furnishings, but it could work. He also told

Ryder that they would be using the upstairs of Betty's Dinor as a temporary gathering place for the club.

When I saw Emma arrive at the explosion sight, my heart ached and I wanted to run to her. I wanted to make sure that she was ok. I hated being away from her, and I could only hope that when this was all over, she would understand and forgive me for the things that I'd done. It took all the restraint I had not to show myself right then and there and let her know that I was still alive. I wanted to hold her and kiss her and tell her that I loved her. But I couldn't. I had to remain hidden. At least she had Hawk and Honey. It was comforting to know that she had people to lean on. More importantly, they were people I could trust. They were there for her and I knew they would take good care of her. I knew I shouldn't have left those flowers for her, but I just needed her to know that everything would be ok. *I wonder if she got them yet?* It was the only option I had right now. I needed to leave her alone until I got all this shit straightened out. *Fuck! This is going to be so much harder than I originally thought when I came up with this godforsaken plan. But, if it all works out, we will all be better off.*

CHAPTER 3

Emma

A few hours later I pulled up to what was left of the Knights' clubhouse. I saw several people digging through the rubble, most of whom were members of the club. *Thank God,* I thought to myself, *they aren't all dead.* I imagined they were looking for anything that they could salvage, but from what I could see from my car, they weren't going to have much luck. Part of the building still stood: the half where Caden's room had been. The other half of the building was completely demolished—it was nothing but stone, broken-up wood, and glass shards.

I canvassed the people, looking for anyone that I knew or recognized, hoping to spot Caden—but he wasn't there, and nobody looked familiar to me. Then I spotted Rebel. I got out of my car and walked toward him. When I got closer, I said, "Oh my gosh, Rebel, what's happened? Did anyone get hurt? Are you ok? Where's Caden?"

I spouted off the questions so fast; I didn't give him a chance to answer. But when I stopped he still didn't speak. He didn't answer for a long time, looking at me as if he was looking at a ghost. He hesitantly said, "How are you here? We thought you were dead." He paused briefly and then added, "Never mind me, are *you* ok?" Before I could say a word to him, he gave me a hug and added, "Emma, I'm so sorry. I was supposed to protect you." He looked devastated. I felt bad for him. None of this was his fault, yet he was carrying the burden on his shoulders.

"Rebel, stop that. I am fine. You did everything you could to protect me. As to how I am here ... Mark let me go yesterday. I came here first, but nobody was here. I went back to my apartment and hoped to find a voice mail or a note, but there was nothing. I came back today, hoping that I would find someone here so I could get some answers as to what's going on. Where's Caden?"

He wouldn't look at me. Something was going on, and I had a feeling I wasn't going to like it. *Where is Caden? Why can't Rebel look me in the eye? Has my worst nightmare come true?*

Just then Hawk walked up looking pretty solemn. "Emma," he asked, seeming confused, "you're alive?"

"Yes, I am. Why is everyone so surprised to see me? I would have thought that Mark had let you all know that he released me. Actually, I assumed Caden or the club had something to do with it somehow."

"Nobody told us that you had been released. Nobody told us that you were still alive. We just assumed you both didn't survive." He quickly stopped talking, as if he was saying more than he should.

What did he mean by "you both?" Surely he didn't mean Caden. "I came to see Ice."

He looked at me hesitantly, seeming uncertain of what to say next. He looked over to Rebel and they had an unspoken conversation as if I wasn't even there. I was really starting to worry. Where was Caden?

"Emma, I'm guessing that you don't know," Hawk said.

"Don't know what?" I asked. He was starting to scare me.

He took a step closer to me and motioned for me to walk with him. He looked back at Rebel, hesitated for a moment, and then continued on walking. I followed. "I'm not sure what happened to you, and I have to say I am a bit surprised to see you here."

"Actually, I doubt that you would believe everything that happened to me. I am having trouble believing it myself," I replied.

"Perhaps once we get this mess straightened out," he said, glancing around at the destruction around him, "we can talk and you can fill me in on the details."

His small talk was all well and good, but I was done with the idle chitchat. "Hawk, where's Ice?" I asked again, frustrated. There was something he wasn't telling me.

"Emma, sweetheart, I'm really sorry to have to tell you this, but Ice is gone."

I had prepared myself for those words, but after actually hearing them coming from Hawk, I could not accept them. It just couldn't be true. I stopped walking and turned toward Hawk and said, "What do you mean he's gone? Where did he go?"

"Emma, I don't think you understand. He didn't *go* anywhere ... he's gone, sweetheart."

My heart stopped. I couldn't move. I couldn't think. I was losing my grip on reality, falling into a darkness that I knew I would never emerge from. My last thought was of Caden before everything went black.

When I came to, I was lying in the back of a van parked in what was left of the Knights' clubhouse parking lot. Hawk and Honey were hovering over me like worried parents. I couldn't understand what had happened. *Why am I lying in the back of this van? Where is Caden?* Then, like a ton of bricks being flung at me all at once, reality hit me and I remembered. I remembered the kidnapping, the destruction of the clubhouse, and the last thing that Hawk had told me. Ice was dead. Ice was dead. My Cade was dead. The tears began to flow uncontrollably and I started having trouble breathing. Hawk and Honey both encouraged me to take deep breaths. They said I would feel better if I let in as much oxygen as I could into my lungs. They were right; taking deep breaths helped. When my breathing got under control, I turned to Hawk and asked, "What happened?"

He looked as if he hadn't slept in days. I hadn't realized that before, but now that I got a closer look at him, I could see the worry and sadness in his eyes. He said, "Emma, I don't know much more than you do." He looked over at Honey and continued, "Honey saw him last, and most of the information I've gotten has been from her."

I turned to Honey. "Where is he? What happened?"

Reluctantly, Honey replied, "I don't know. He was frantic trying to find you. He was on the phone in the clubhouse when he realized there was a bomb and he yelled for everyone to get out. When he was sure that everyone was out of the building, he left and the building blew. We all just stood in disbelief for what seemed like an eternity. After he was sure everyone was whole, he made a call. I don't know who he called and was too far away to make out what was said. After he finished the call he walked over to me and told me to tell Hawk what had happened, that he'd found you, and that he had to go."

"Did he say anything else?" I asked, irritated—no, not irritated. I was jealous that she was the last person to see him, to talk to him ... but at least someone did see him and speak to him. *I guess I should be thankful for that. Does he know that I love him? I can't remember, did I tell him? No! No! He's not dead. I refuse to believe it.*

She hesitated for a minute, and then glanced over at Hawk as if asking his permission to reveal more. Hawk nodded. She continued, "He said that he would be back."

Well, then why are they thinking that he is dead? They have all lost their minds. "Then you all are wrong!" I exclaimed. "You all think you know Caden, but you don't. None of you know him like I do. If Caden Jackson says he will be back, then you can be damn sure he will!" I was frustrated and angry. These two were probably two of the closest people to him, and here I was trying to convince them that he would come back. Or was I actually trying to convince myself? *No! He can't be gone. If he were gone, I wouldn't feel his presence. And I still feel him!*

"Emma, you are not seeing the big picture here. I think I know him pretty well. The man I know would have taken care of his business and then returned to his club where he was needed most. He wouldn't have left us to pick up the pieces without him." As much as I hated to admit it, Hawk was right. Caden would have rescued me, taken care of Mark, and hightailed it back to his club where he was needed. Hawk continued, "Emma, I know what you're feeling, sweetheart. I want him here too; he was my best friend. But I think you're grasping at straws, trying to change what is real. I'm sorry, sweetheart, but he's gone."

Just then Rebel walked up. "Hawk, I'm heading out to get Ari. Do you need anything before I go?"

Oh my God, Ari. I totally forgot about her. I said, "Does Ari know?" Rebel shook his head. "Who's gonna tell her?"

"I am," Rebel said, sadly.

"Rebel, I have not seen Ari in a long time, but I think it would be better if I told her. We grew up together, and I believe she always looked up to me as a big sister."

Hawk shook his head. "Actually, Emma, she needs Rebel now." He turned back toward Rebel and said, "Reb, you go. Be careful and bring our girl back safe and sound."

"You got it, Hawk."

I interrupted again. "But Hawk ..."

"Emma, please. Don't interfere with club business."

When did Ari become club business? I thought to myself.

Hawk continued, "Trust me on this; I know what I'm doing. Ari and Reb are very close. He is whom she will need. It's what Ice would have wanted."

Well, hell. I guess I don't know either one of them as well as I thought. I nodded in agreement.

CHAPTER 4

Caden

Rebel was the only club member that I had talked to since I disappeared. He knew everything. I had to have someone on the inside who knew what I was up to and to explain things to Hawk when the time was right. Plus, he had to take care of Ari. He had to assure her that I was ok, and she wouldn't believe anyone but him. Those two had an obvious connection, but neither of them would commit to the other. I thought, *Maybe after all the dust settles and things get back to normal those two will finally admit their feelings to each other and me.* The tension between them could be overbearing at times.

But I had more important things to worry about. I needed to call Rebel. He was probably almost in Gettysburg by now. I dialed his number and he answered on the first ring. "Yeah?"

"Hey, it's me. Are you on your way to get Ari?"

"Sure am. Are you sure you want me to tell her that you're still alive?" he asked.

"Yes. She will be able to play along for the others and I need her to be convincing. I am guessing that Hawk, Honey, and Emma have just realized that I am alive. They've been to Grayson's house and seen my handiwork."

"Ice, man, you are one crazy fucker."

"He fucked with the wrong person. He threatened my girl, my club, and my sister! Fucker deserved everything he got and more."

"I don't know, man, something just doesn't sit right with me about all this."

"Reb, trust me. I know what I am doing. By the time I resurface, it will be safe for our club and our families. I'm tired of this shit," I said.

"I know, boss, I do. I just hate having to keep up this charade. Do you really think the girls can pull it off?"

"I do. Women are amazing actresses. They can do it. I'm more worried about you and Hawk," I said with a laugh. It was true. I knew if anyone would slip about me still being alive, it would one of them.

"You don't need to worry about us. I got this, and so does Hawk. He doesn't know I know yet, but when I get back, he will." He paused for a moment then added, "So, do you want me to take Ari to your house?"

"Yes, I think that would be good." The house was out of the way, and very few people even knew I had a house outside of the clubhouse. I never stayed there. I thought about it and then added, "I want you to get Emma moved into the house as well. I don't want her in that apartment alone anymore. Especially now."

"You got it, boss. Anything else?"

"Yes. Honey. Bring her to the house too. She has no other place to go and I don't want her wasting money on a hotel until we have a new clubhouse. She has always had a home with us and I want her to continue to know that."

"Anything else?"

"Nope, I think we are good for now. You got anything you want to say to me?" Rebel had had a thing for my kid sister I think from day one, but he had never acted on it. I believed Ari liked him too. Before she left for school, they were always together. I thought for sure they would hook up, but they never did. I was always trying to get him to admit it to me, but he never would. Sometimes, I just liked fucking with his head.

"One more thing. I'm almost in Gettysburg. It's roughly 4:00 pm. Got any idea where she might be?"

I laughed. "And here I expected you to know that. Don't mess with me, buddy, I know you keep tabs on her."

"I don't know what you are talking about," he said defensively.

"Look, man, I know you have a thing for my sister, and I also know that you struggle with the age difference and how your relationship affects me. Believe me, I've been down that road myself with Emma. You are my brother and I trust you with her. But let me tell you—you fucking hurt her, and I will kill you. Got it?"

"Got it!"

"Ok, now go get my sister and bring her home safe. There is nobody else I trust her safety with more than you," I said and then hung up the phone.

Emma

I was beginning to feel ill. The news about Caden, fainting, and all this devastation around me ... it was all getting to me. I needed to be alone. I had to process everything, and being hovered over by Hawk and Honey was not helping. There were too many connections to Caden here.

"I need to go," I said.

"Are you sure, sweetheart? You are still looking a little pale," Hawk said. "You can stay here as long as you like."

"Thank you, Hawk, I really appreciate that. But I need to be alone for a while." As I started to get up out of the van, I turned back toward Hawk and asked weakly, "Are you really sure he is dead?"

Hawk looked confused by my question. "I am."

"Hawk, just hear me out for a minute." I took a second to get my thoughts together and then said; "Caden didn't contact any of you after he left the clubhouse. So nobody has seen nor heard from him. Correct?"

"Yes," Honey replied. "Like I said before, I am pretty sure I was the last person he spoke to in the club."

"Ok, so if nobody has heard from him and nobody has talked to him, what makes you both so sure he is dead. Maybe he has some grand plan to fix this? Maybe he is still with Mark? And, although I am stating the obvious here, let me add, you don't have his body."

Hawk looked over to Honey and said, "She's got a point." He turned back toward me and said, "I do still believe, however, that if he were alive he would've contacted us."

"I agree," I said, "But what if he can't? What if he is still being held captive in the same place that Mark held me, only in a different room? I mean think about this. If he had gone to rescue me, wouldn't the most likely place he would go is where I was. I even yelled for him when I left in case he was there. I wanted him to know that Mark was letting me go. If he was planning any type of attack against Grayson, he would have waited until he knew I was safe."

"Well shit Emma, I didn't think of any of that." Hawk replied. Then he added, "You shame me. I should've thought this through more thoroughly."

"Well you did have other things on your mind, like a blown up clubhouse." I stated sarcastically. Then I added, "I think we should look for him first before we pronounce him dead. And I know where you can start." I said proudly.

Hawk immediately looked up to me in surprise. I don't think he realized that I knew where I was after I'd been released. "How could you possibly know that?"

"Because I have a pretty good idea where I was being held."

"So you know where Grayson was keeping you?" he asked hopefully.

"I don't know the exact address, but I have a good idea. I bet if we retraced my steps, I could find it again," I said encouragingly.

"What do you mean retrace your steps?" he asked.

"When Mark released me, he basically just kicked me out. I didn't have a car, and I had no idea where I was. So I started walking until I came across a gas station and used their phone to call a cab."

Looking hopeful, he said, "Look, Emma, I realize that you have been through a horrific ordeal, but you could really help us out a lot

36

if you and I sat down somewhere and you told me everything that has transpired over the last 48 hours."

I nodded. He was right. As much as I wanted to be left alone, if there was anything I knew that could lead us to Caden, I was willing to put my own needs aside and help all that I could. "Yes, I will do what I can to help you," I said.

Hawk smiled. It was the first time I had seen him smile since I had gotten there. "Thank you. I'm sure this will be difficult for you, but any information you could provide would help a lot." He paused for a moment and then added, "Why don't we get out of here? We'll go grab a cup of coffee and we can talk. I've been working on a new location for the club but it will be weeks until it is ready. I've secured the vacant space above Betty's Dinor until we have something permanent. We can talk there."

"Ok, that sounds nice."

He turned back toward Honey. "Why don't you join us? I think having you there will help Emma." Honey glanced over to me and I nodded, confirming that I agreed with Hawk. I did want her there.

CHAPTER 5

Emma

With Honey riding on the back of his bike, Hawk followed me to Betty's Dinor. When we arrived, we found a table in the back where we could have some privacy. The waitress approached and asked, "What'll you have?"

Hawk ordered for all of us: two black coffees, one with cream. He looked over to me and asked, "Do you want anything to eat?"

I shook my head no. The last thing I could do right now was eat.

Hawk waited for the waitress to leave and then turned to me again and asked, "Emma, are you ready?" I nodded and he added, "Why don't you start from the beginning."

"Ok, let me think for a minute," I said. I took a deep breath and began, "Rebel and I had just gotten back from the grocery store. No, wait—I need to go back a little further. At the grocery store, there was a man there with a devil tattoo on the back of his neck that seemed to be hovering around me. I actually bumped into him, and when Rebel came up and asked me what was wrong, the man was gone. I told Rebel about it, and when we left we saw a Harley in the parking lot. He asked me to watch the bike as we left to make sure it stayed parked. It did. When we got back to the house, we started to unload groceries."

Hawk interrupted me and asked, "Did anything look out of the ordinary when you got back to the house?"

I thought for a moment and then replied, "No, nothing that I noticed."

Looking disappointed, he said, "Ok, go on."

"So, Rebel was going into the house as I was coming out. I got to the car and started to grab a couple of bags, then everything went dark. The next thing I remember is being in a dark room, tied to a bed." I stopped. I really didn't know if I could go on. When Hawk had asked me to tell him everything that happened, I hadn't thought it would be that difficult ... but now that I'd gotten to the hard part, I realized that I may not be able to continue.

Hawk sensed my hesitation and reached for my arm. Laying his hand on my arm, he said, "Emma, I can only imagine what you have experienced during this ordeal. But, sweetheart, I really need to know everything. If we are ever going to find out what's happened to Ice, you need to tell me everything."

I knew he was right. In my head, I could tell him everything ... but saying the words out loud was going to be the hard part. In my heart, I knew Caden was still alive. I also knew that what I was about to tell Hawk would help us find him. So, I decided it was time to put on my big-girl panties and do what I needed to do for Caden. He was prepared to give his life for me; this was the least I could do for him.

I paused briefly and continued. "As I said, I woke up in a very dark room, naked and tied to a bed. Mark was there, and for the longest time, he would not speak to me. He only laughed. His laugh sounded as if it came from Satan himself. It terrified me, and I don't think I will ever forget it. I was really scared and the only thing that kept me sane was the hope that Caden or the club would find me. But nobody ever came."

"Emma, did Mark rape you?" Hawk asked hesitantly. I could see the concern in his eyes, and I could see why Caden trusted and respected this man so much. It was clear that he was genuine and real and it made me trust him as well.

I shook my head. "No, he didn't. He tried, but when I refused to fight back it made him angry. So angry that he stopped and left the room."

"Oh thank God!" Honey exclaimed.

Hawk reached over to me to place his hand on my shoulder. "I'm thankful that he didn't rape you. You're gonna have enough scars from this ordeal to handle, you don't need any more on your plate." He paused briefly then added, "I assume the bruises on your face are from him?" Hawk asked.

"Yes, he hit me in the face several times. I tried very hard to remain coherent, but it was difficult. I believe over the course of the time that I was there, which I am guessing was a little over 24 hours, that I went in and out of consciousness several times."

"Did he give you any reasons as to why he was doing this?"

"Yes," I replied. "He was very calculated in his reason, mentioning that he had Brianne worked over because she was threatening to tell me everything about him. He never went into details as to what that was, so I don't know what he didn't want me to know, but that he wanted to teach her a lesson." I stopped to remember some of the things he said and then added; "He also said that when I ran to Caden for help it only moved his plan along faster. When I asked him what plan, he said that he wanted to take back from Caden all that Caden took from him. None of that made any sense to me. I didn't have any clue what he was talking about— for all I knew, they had never met. I'm afraid that this was all my fault."

"Did he say anything else?" Hawk asked.

I thought about it for a minute, then added, "He said that he was going to break me; that he was going to use me over and over again and then send me back to Caden and the club that rejected him. I didn't get the impression from him that he'd had Brianne killed, so I think she is still alive. If this is all my fault Hawk, I'm so sorry." I looked at them both in shame and started to cry. Hawk placed his hand on mine in an attempt to console me, but it didn't help. I believed what I said to be true. It was all my fault.

Hawk asked, "Do you know what it was that he was trying to hide from you?"

I pulled myself together and shook my head. "No, I have no idea. He never said any more about it and when I asked he would just tell me to shut up."

He then asked, "Can you remember anything else?"

I thought about it for a minute, then replied, "Yes, he said that he knew about my relationship with Caden longer than he had known me. I really didn't think about it much then, but looking back now, I find that very odd. Caden and I grew up together. How would Mark know anything about my childhood?"

"Not so odd, Emma. Based on what you have said, I think there is more to this than just a jealous boyfriend who lost his girl to the big bad biker. I believe there is a past connection between Ice and Mark that we don't know about. It could be the driving force for all of this. You and Brianne just got caught in the middle. So, please, stop blaming yourself. I believe we'll find out more once we get to where you were being held." He paused briefly then added, "Anything else?"

"He showed me a video that was recorded the other night."

"A video?" he asked.

"Yes, it was a video of a party at your clubhouse. Caden was with another woman. Mark said that he wanted me to see what kind of man I was involved with." I looked over to Honey and said, "I think it may have been you dressed up as me, but Mark never said anything to that effect. He just wanted me to think that Caden was cheating on me."

Honey looked at me apologetically. "It was me, but I was just a decoy, Emma. The club wanted the Satans to think that you were at the clubhouse. They didn't want them to know that Caden had sent you away. I promise, nothing happened."

"I know, Honey, but thanks for saying it. At first, I felt that Caden had abandoned me. I felt that I had nothing left and that if I got out alive, I still would have nothing 'cause I had lost Cade to another woman. I was praying that Mark would just get it over with, 'cause at that point, I was sure he was going to rape me and then kill me. I had given up. I think that is what saved me. I went completely still; I was lifeless and had stopped crying. I had no more fight in me. When I just laid there, silent, not even crying anymore, that's when Mark got angry and stormed out of the room. He left that video on and I watched it over and over. After viewing it several times, I realized that it was you with Caden." I glanced over to Honey, shrugged, and continued, "Eventually I fell asleep or lost consciousness, I am not really sure which. When I came to, I heard talking out in the hallway, but the only voice I heard was Mark's. I realized he was talking to himself, but not just in the normal way people talk to themselves. No, Mark was actually arguing with himself. It was very creepy and I had never seen him do that before. He stormed into the room, still talking. He untied me and threw my clothes at me. He ordered me to get dressed and get out."

"That's it?" Honey asked, surprised.

"Yeah, he basically just threw me out. That's why I had to find my way back home."

A look of realization came upon Hawk's face and he said, "So that is how you know where he kept you. Can you take us there?"

I nodded. "Sure, I can try. I walked for several blocks until I found a gas station and called a cab from there. The clerk at the gas station gave me the address for the cab company. Wait, I think I still have it." I rummaged through my purse and found it. "Here it is!" I handed the paper to Hawk. "The lady at the gas station gave me money for a cab to get home. I saved the address so that I could go back and repay her."

"Wattsburg? What in the hell was he doing there?" Hawk asked, surprised.

I shook my head. "I don't know. I remember when I left I looked back at the place that held so much horror for me and couldn't believe that it was a quaint little house in a residential neighborhood. It was kinda eerie, knowing what lived behind that door."

Hawk looked disgusted. I wasn't sure if his disgust was directed at me or if it came from the story I had just told him. I couldn't fully buy into Hawk's theory that I had gotten caught in the middle of something bigger between Cade and Mark. I still felt to blame. But I couldn't change what was done. I could only do my part to help fix what could be fixed.

Hawk asked, "Emma, are you up to going back to Wattsburg?"

I didn't hesitate. "Absolutely!" I was sure that going back there would get us one step closer to finding Caden. I refused to believe he was dead.

Hawk called the waitress over, got our check, and paid our bill. We headed out to find Mark's house.

Honey and I followed Hawk back to his house. He left his bike and we all continued in my car, but I let Hawk drive. About forty-five minutes later, we pulled up to the gas station in Wattsburg where the clerk had helped me. We all got out of the car and Hawk asked, "Do you remember how you got here?"

I stood in the parking lot for what seemed like several minutes looking around. Finally, I recognized the street that I'd walked down. "There!" I said. "I came from that direction."

"Ok, let's go," Hawk said.

"Wait, let me do something first. I'll be real quick." I ran into the gas station and saw the lady that had helped me yesterday at the counter. She was just finishing up with a customer when she spotted me.

"You're back!" she said, surprised.

I pulled a $50 out of my wallet and handed it to her. "Thank you so much for helping me yesterday. I really appreciate it." The look on her face was one of total surprise. I don't think she ever expected to see that money again.

She smiled at me and said, "Thank you." She paused for a moment, then added, "Are you ok?"

"Yes, I am. Thank you again."

I walked out of the door and headed back to my car. Hawk and Honey were inside waiting for me. I got in the car and we headed down the road that I'd pointed out before. Hawk drove until we got to the next intersection. He stopped and waited. I looked around again but didn't see anything that caught my eye as familiar, and said, "Go straight." At the next intersection, he stopped again. I looked and remembered the beautiful dogwood that rested in the yard of the house on the corner to my left. That was where I'd turned. I turned to Hawk and said, "Turn right." This continued for about five more minutes and suddenly I realized I was on the street where Mark's house was. "Drive slower, Hawk. We're almost there." Hawk slowed down and the house came into view. "That's the one. Right there, on the left. The one with the front porch and rocking chairs."

Hawk drove past it to the next block and parked the car. As he started to get out of the car, he turned to Honey and I and said, "You both stay here for now until I check things out. I mean it, ladies! I don't need to be worrying about either of you right now. Stay put!" He reached into his cut and pulled out a gun, turned the safety off, and cocked it. He started walking toward the house.

After Hawk left, I turned to Honey and said, "This is driving me crazy. How in the hell does he expect us to just wait here?"

"I know, I agree, but he's right, he doesn't need to be worrying about us too. Let's let him do what he needs to do and he'll come back for us," Honey replied.

I grunted in disapproval but didn't say another word. We just sat there in agonizing silence.

About fifteen minutes later, Hawk returned to the car. He got in and said, "I don't think anyone is there. I'm gonna call the boys for backup. We're going to go in." He got on the phone and began speaking to Ryder. He asked him to bring three or four brothers and gave him the address. After he hung up, he got back out of the car. Leaning in the window, he asked, "You ladies coming?"

Honey and I didn't hesitate; we both proceeded to get out of the car. I wasn't sure that I really wanted to go back in the house again, but if it would help Cade, then I would do it. We walked back down the block to the house. When we got there, Hawk walked up on the porch and rang the bell. I guessed that he was checking again, just to make sure that nobody was home. He waited a few seconds and when nobody answered, he tried the door. It was locked. He looked at both Honey and I and we could see the frustration on his face. He came down from the porch and walked around toward the back, where he found a side door. He walked up to it and tried to open it. It swung open.

He turned back to us and said, "Wait here." Hesitantly, he walked into the house. He was gone for about five minutes. When he came back, he just said, "Come on."

Honey and I walked up the steps to the door. When we walked in, the hair on the back of my neck started to prickle. The memories of what I had endured in this house were very fresh in my mind and a part of me wanted to turn around and run home. But I had to remember why we were here. Once I thought about Caden and got a clear picture of him in my head, I knew I could go on. We walked through the kitchen, a part of the house that I had not seen when I was here two nights ago. The kitchen looked perfectly normal; nobody would believe the evil that lives here. We got to a rather long hallway with several closed doors running down it. Hawk opened the first door on the left to reveal a bathroom. He went to the second door on the left and opened it. I was afraid that it was the room that I'd been held in, but looking in, it was fair to assume we had found Mark's bedroom. His closet was open and clothes were hanging in it. There was a bed and a dresser and an open door that led to the bathroom that we'd just passed. *Why didn't I know that he had this house? I dated the man for four years and was engaged to him, but the only residence of his that I knew about was his penthouse in Erie.*

Hawk started to check out the room, going through Mark's things on the dresser, opening dresser drawers, and scoping out his closet. He didn't react to anything he was seeing, so I assumed he hadn't found anything that could help. We walked out of Mark's room and looked at the three closed doors across the hall. I knew one of them had to be *the* room. The prickling started again, but I brushed it off. I had to get through this.

Hawk opened the first door. It was clear that Mark had used this room as an office. He had several file cabinets, a desk, and of course a chair. On the desk was a laptop. Hawk said, "I think we might find something here that will help us. When the boys get here, I will have Dbag check out the computer and the files." He left the door open and moved on to the next.

When he opened the next door, the odor hit me first. This was the room. I followed Hawk into the room. It was dark and eerie, looking like it belonged in a dungeon. I'd never seen this room with a light on and couldn't believe what I was seeing. The walls were painted black. Even the window had black curtains drawn across it, which dimmed the only outside light entering the room. There was a bed in the center of the room with ropes and chains attached all around it. Hanging on the wall were various whips, canes, and belts. *Oh God, what crazy shit is he involved with?* In all the time that I'd known Mark, I'd never seen this side of him.

Honey followed me into the room and shrieked, "Holy fuck, Emma! Is this the room that he held you in?"

Quietly, I replied, "Yes, I believe it is."

She walked over to me and hugged me, whispering, "I'm so sorry."

"It's over now. We need to concentrate on finding Caden." Both Honey and Hawk looked at each other, worried. I knew they thought he was dead, that we were going to find his body. But I refused to believe it. I would know if he was dead. I would feel it.

"What is that God-awful smell?" Hawk asked.

"Hell if I know," said Honey, "but it smells like piss." She was right. It did smell like piss. It was disgusting and made my stomach turn.

Hawk added, "I need to get out of this room. I'll have the boys go through shit in here when they get here."

After we all left the room, Hawk closed the door behind us. He approached the last door and opened it. From what I could see, it opened to a stairway that led to the basement. "What the fuck!" Hawk yelled.

I didn't understand why he was yelling, but then suddenly the odor hit me. It was bad enough that it overpowered the lingering smell from the last room. With both smells combined, I thought I was going to vomit. The odor that came from this room was one hundred times worse than the room we'd just left. Hawk walked back to the kitchen and rummaged around in the drawers. I didn't know what he was doing, but when he pulled out three towels it became clear. He handed Honey and me one apiece, covered his nose with the third one, and proceeded to descend down the stairs with Honey and me close behind. When we got to the bottom, Hawk flipped the light switch. We all stood there in horror. What we saw before us was more blood and gore than I could imagine from the worst murder scene.

We were indeed in the basement of the house. It wasn't a very big area at all; it was only a partial basement. In the center of the room was a metal table. There were all types of surgical instruments scattered on the table, all of which were drenched in blood. Blood dripped off the table into a puddle below. Some of it had dried, but there was so much of it that it all had not dried. But it was definitely fresh ... as in the last 48 hours fresh. For the first time since Hawk told me that Caden was dead, I actually feared for his life.

Hanging from a hook on the rafters was a body. It was in the shadows and we could not make out who it was until we got closer. *Oh dear God, please let that not be Caden*, I prayed to myself. Hawk approached the body, examined it as best he could and then asked, "Emma, please. I need you to come here."

Hesitantly, I approached the body. I was terrified that it was Caden, but as I got closer, I could see that it wasn't. When I was standing next to Hawk, he asked, "Is this Mark Grayson?"

At first, relief washed over me like a tidal wave, and I nodded. "Yes." *Thank you, God. I knew it; Caden is still alive.* I was relieved that it was not Caden. But then, I took another look at Mark's mutilated body and thought, *who could have done this to him? Could another human being be that savage? Of course they could, but who?* And then, the worst possible feeling filled my heart. *This was my fault! Mark died this way because of me.*

Hawk shook his head in disbelief, glanced back at Honey, and said, "Ice is back."

"Hawk, no, please say that Ice didn't do this," Honey pleaded. I didn't understand what they were talking about. As far as I was concerned, this proved that Cade was alive. Caden wouldn't do this to another person, I was sure of that. So why would they think that? And more importantly, why weren't they happy?

"It's his signature work. Grayson has been tortured, and flames have been carved into his chest. Ice did this, I'm sure of it," Hawk confirmed.

"Fuck!" Honey replied.

I said, "What's going on? He's alive! Why aren't you both happy about this? Mark is dead and Cade is alive!" Waiting for them to respond, I thought, *but why didn't he come back to his club or me?* Something wasn't adding up. When neither Honey nor Hawk responded, I added, "What's going on, you two? What aren't you telling me?"

"Emma, let's go back upstairs away from this mess and wait for the boys. Then I'll try to explain," Hawk replied. I turned to go back up the steps, Honey and Hawk following me. Now that there was no worry of Mark returning, we all proceeded to the kitchen and sat down at the table. Hawk grabbed my hand and said, "Emma, there are things about Ice that you don't know. I don't believe he is the same person that you grew up with." He hesitated for a moment, then continued, "Things have happened in his past that I believe have changed him."

All right, Captain Obvious, just get to the point. His beating around the bush was pissing me off. I knew Caden had changed, and so had I. What did that matter, and what did that have to do with the dead body in the basement?

"Hawk, I don't mean to be rude, but I know he's changed. I know he is not the boy that I knew as a child. But really, what does all that have to do with the dead psychopath in the basement?"

"I don't think you are understanding me. I'm trying to be delicate, but I see that's not working. So, I'm just gonna lay it out for you." He paused for a moment, looked over to Honey—for support, I guess—then continued. "Caden—no, not Caden ... Let me rephrase that. Ice is responsible for that bloodbath in the basement."

I immediately shook my head. "No! No, Caden would never do that!" I yelled.

"I know, you are right. Caden wouldn't have done that. But Ice would. He's done this before. I've seen this same type of handiwork before and Ice confirmed it himself that he did it."

"Are you trying to tell me that Caden—Ice, whoever—tortured Mark and murdered him?"

"Yes, that is exactly what I am telling you," Hawk replied.

"Why? Why would you think that?"

Just then, we heard the roar of several Harleys. The rest of the club had arrived. Hawk got up from the table and met the boys outside. A few minutes later, Ryder, Spike, Dbag, and Doc walked into the kitchen. They nodded to Honey and I. Then Ryder asked Hawk, "Where do you need us?"

"Go down that hallway. There are several rooms that need to be searched, and the basement needs cleaned up. I'm gonna warn you, it's not pretty down there," Hawk said. Ryder nodded and he and the others proceeded down the hall to the search the house. Hawk watched as he walked down the hallway, then said, "Where were we?"

"You were about to tell me why you think Caden is a cold-blooded killer," I stated angrily.

Hawk sighed took a deep breath and began. "After Ace was killed, Caden took the retaliation for Ace's death solely upon himself. When the club was sent in to clean up his mess, Ice told me everything that had happened ..."

CHAPTER 6

Caden (Three years ago)

The only person who was ever a real father to me was dead. I knew I would never forget how he, a total stranger at the time, took me under his wing, taught me what I needed to know to make a life for Ari and myself, and treated me as if I was his own son. Ace had never let me down, until now. *How could that crazy bastard get himself killed? I'm so fucking pissed at him! But I'm more pissed at that lowlife Satan who got the best of him. That Satan is going to pay. It's time to get my revenge. It's time to claim the blood that was stolen from this club.*

After Ace's death, I'd been voted in as the new club president. I could have taken advantage of that position and pulled the whole club into my revenge, but ... not this time. I knew they believed that this retaliation was theirs; after all, Ace was their president. But this fight was mine. Ace's revenge was mine. I wasn't going to share that with any of them. Maybe it made me a bad president. Maybe I was just selfish. Either way, I was getting this shit done. Every last Satan involved in his death was going to pay.

The Satans had messed with my town and my club for the last time. All I wanted to do was hunt and kill those fuckers one by one.

I parked my bike outside Dirty Dick's. The Satans loved that hole in the ground. Personally, I thought the place was a dump. I waited and I watched. It was a slow night at the bar: there were only three cars in the parking lot, along with seven Harleys, including mine. I was the only one in the parking lot except for a guy, who looked to be rather young, sitting on one of the Harleys. I didn't think he was a member of the Satans; he wasn't wearing their colors, or even a cut for that matter, and his bike was parked away from the other five. I temporarily got lost wondering who he was and why he was there. I had to stop myself. I couldn't do that shit now. I needed to focus and take care of what I came for.

As I got off my bike I reached in my saddlebag and pulled out my KG9 and my Glock. Fully armed, I walked toward the door. Next thing I knew, someone behind me called, "Ice, wait."

What the fuck? I'm carrying two guns and this idiot calls after me. And the little fucker knows my name. How does he fuckin' know my name? Didn't anyone ever teach this him that you don't approach a guy carrying two guns, especially a biker? Fuck, I really hate stupid people and will never understand the shit they do. I don't need this now. I turned to see who was calling after me, assuming it was the guy on his bike. Sure enough, I was right. He was walking towards me with a hopeful look on his face.

"Look, man, you better get out of here. Something is about to go down that you don't want to be a part of."

I turned to leave again and again he called after me. "Wait, Ice, you don't understand. I do want to be a part of this. I know who you are and I have a pretty good idea why you are here." Before I could shut him down again, he hurriedly continued on, "I know you are the president of the Knights of Silence MC and I also know that this place is not your normal hangout. This is Satans' territory, and there is only one reason why you would be here." After hearing him speak more, I realized this kid had a bit of an

Irish accent.

I took a step closer to him to get a better look at him. "And why would you want to get involved in this shit?" I asked curiously. He intrigued me.

"Because I know what they did. I know they killed Ace."

"How do you know who Ace is?" He'd piqued my curiosity again. I knew I shouldn't be engaging him in conversation, but there was something about him that was strangely familiar.

"Ace sent me to find you. I've been watching you and your club for a while now. I can help you."

What the fuck? How did this guy know Ace? I laughed. "You're just a kid. How do you think you can help me?"

"You're planning on going in there and taking down as many Satans as you can. I doubt you can do it alone. But with my help, we can wipe out every Satan in there." He sounded so confident, and I realized why he seemed familiar. He reminded me of myself when I was his age.

I laughed again and started to walk toward the door. He grabbed my arm. "Please, let me help you. I owe Ace that much."

I could see desperation in his eyes. Again, that desperation reminded me of myself. After my parents had been killed and I had nothing, I had that desperation. I'm sure Ace saw it when I asked him for a job that day. He took a chance on me.

The kid then repeated, "Ace told me to find you." This kid knew Ace. I didn't have time at the moment to find out why, I just knew that I had to take a chance on him. Ace had trusted him for some reason, therefore I trusted him. I questioned myself briefly, wondering if it was fair of me to put him in a position where he would most likely get killed. After a second, I decided: fuck it. I was probably gonna get killed too.

"Fine, it's your neck. Can you shoot?" I asked.
"Hell, yeah!" he said as he walked over to his bike. He grabbed a KG9 from his saddlebag and said, "I'm pretty good with a knife, too."

Holy shit! I looked the gun over closely. It was perfect: street-converted, full auto, no marks. Where the fuck did he get that? Ace could sure as hell pick 'em, and this kid was no exception. It was obvious he knew his shit.

"Ok, then ... let's go. The only thing I'm gonna tell you is shoot to disarm, not kill. If they are wearing Satan colors, they get shot—but don't kill anyone until I tell you. I need answers, so I can't have them all dead at once. I've got plans for these assholes. Got it?"

"Yes, sir!"

I shook my head. This kid was too fucking eager. He definitely reminded me of myself. I had to laugh at the irony of it all. "By the way, what's your name?" I asked.

"Balefire."

What the fuck kind of name is that?

As if he knew what I was thinking, he added, "It's Irish."

No shit, Sherlock. "Well then ... looks like I got myself a *rebel* Irishman."

We walked into the bar quietly. The doorway was dark and off to the side. It didn't appear that anyone noticed us at all. I scoped around the room. Other than a waitress, a bartender, and five Satans sitting smugly at the bar, the place was empty. Perfect. I wanted to do damage, but I didn't need any collateral damage. I realized I was in control of this situation. Fear no longer existed and I knew without a doubt that the kid and I were going to walk out of there very much alive.

The waitress walked by us and I touched her on the arm. She turned toward me and I said quietly, "Sweetheart, I suggest you get your pretty little ass out of here. Take the bartender and anyone else who may be working with you." She looked at me, then at my cut, and then fixated on the guns I was toting. She nodded. She could see that I was there to take care of business and that I had no intention of harming her or any other innocents that worked there. She walked casually over to the bar. I watched patiently as she whispered to the bartender. He nodded and they both went into the back room and hopefully out the door. I turned to the kid. "Ready, Rebel?" He looked at me quizzically. Then, realizing that I had just given him his road name, he nodded.

Guns cocked, we walked directly to the Satans seated at the bar. As I got closer, I could see that we had four patched members and a prospect at our mercy. Shit was about to hit the fan, and I couldn't have been more stoked.

Guns cocked, we walked directly to the Satans seated at the bar. As I got closer, I could see that we had four patched members and a prospect at our mercy. Shit was about to hit the fan, and I couldn't have been more stoked.

"Enjoy your drink, boys, it's about to be your last!" I said as I approached. It was clear that they had no idea that we had even entered the bar. This element of surprise gave us the advantage we needed. With two KG9s and a semi-automatic handgun on them, there was nothing they could do. We quickly shot and disabled everyone of them, and they all fell to the floor in total shock. "Rebel, get their weapons!" He did as he was told as I kept my aim on those fuckers.

Then I asked, "Which one of you fuckers killed Ace?" They were silent. "Come on, boys. I know you all can talk. The way I see it, you have two choices. You can tell me what I want to know, or you can sit there like a bunch of dumbasses and I'll keep shooting until you can't do anything but scream in pain. Either way, I win. So, what's it gonna be?" Again, they were silent. I called over to Rebel, "Hey Reb, what do you think? Should I go for the kneecaps next?"

"Oh yeah, I hear that when you're shot in the kneecaps the pain is unbearable. Grown men will cry like babies," he said. He paused for a moment and then added, "God, I love that sound."

Damn, he loves this shit just as much as I do! It didn't take me long to realize that I liked this kid. I made a mental note to talk to him about prospecting with the club.

One of the Satans said, "Go ahead, you assholes. We're dead anyway!"

Son of a bitch, he thinks that I am just gonna put more bullets in him and make it easy. He doesn't know me very well. I pointed my gun at his knees and fired twice, one shot per knee, dead center in the kneecap. He screamed in pain as the blood poured from his legs. Served him right.

"Who's next?" I asked. I looked at the guy next to the asshole. "You, prospect? Do you want to know what it feels like to get shot in the knees? Do you love your club so much that you'd take a bullet for them?" He shook his head. "Oh, so perhaps he is the smart one of the group. Did you kill Ace?" I asked. He shook his head again. It was pretty sad to see these tough bikers trembling with fear. If I was going to get anyone to give me the intel that I needed, it was gonna be this prospect. It usually doesn't take much for them to crack. "So, tell me, smart guy, who killed Ace?" He didn't say anything. "I'm not gonna ask again!" I stated as I pointed the gun at his knees.

"Ok, ok! I'll tell you!" he yelled. We were finally getting somewhere.

"You weak fucker, you just signed your death warrant!" one of the other members yelled.

Fucking smug asshole. Didn't he realize that they were all about to meet their maker? He pissed me off so much I shot him right between the eyes. One down. Maybe that will teach these assholes to speak only when spoken to.

"Well, rat-boy? Start talking."
The guy hesitated at first. He looked around to his brothers fearfully and then said, "Psycho did it." He glanced guiltily at the guy lying next to him.

Bingo. I've got my man! I walked over to the guy lying next to the prospect and looked at his patch. Sure enough, he was the guy. I dragged him away from the others. I then turned to the kid and said, "Kill them." He shot all four of them point-blank in the chest. "Nice work! Now kid, go outside and wait for me. I've got this." He hesitated. I added, "Go! This guy is mine!" Reluctantly, he turned to leave.

Psycho and I were finally alone. Now it was going to get fun!

CHAPTER 7

Emma (Present day)

Hawk said, "I'll spare you the gory details of what happened to Psycho, but after what you have witnessed in the basement, I'm sure you have pretty good idea." Hawk paused for a moment to let his words sink in. He then continued, "After Ice told us what he did to the Satans, the club took care of the cleanup. When we arrived at Dirty Dick's, what we saw was very similar to the scene we just discovered downstairs. He and Rebel had killed five Satans, torturing the one who'd killed Ace. The last thing he did was carve flames into his chest, just like our friend downstairs."

When he finished, I sat there in disbelief. Sure, Cade had told me that he'd killed people. He'd said it was bad guys killing bad guys for the greater good, or some bullshit like that. He justified it. But this? Could he be cold-blooded enough to torture someone in that way?

Quietly, I asked, "That's why you call him Ice, isn't it?" It all made sense now. And to think that I was naïve enough to believe that he got his name because of his eyes.

Hawk nodded. "Yes. It seems when those that he loves are hurt, something takes over in him and he turns cold. He becomes a predator that you don't want to mess with. You were threatened, and we all know how much he loves you. It only makes sense that he would react like that again."

"What happened after that?" I asked. I wasn't sure I really wanted him to continue his story, but something morbid inside of me had to know.

Hawk continued, "After the massacre, we knew that the Satans would come looking for us. So, we voted to take down the Satans once and for all. We commissioned other Chapters in the area to assist. Anyone who refused was given the opportunity to leave or face punishment. Everyone stayed. I think after hearing what Ice had done, they not only respected him, they feared him. When people fear another person, it gives that person power over them and at times can be a bad thing. But in this situation, it worked to our advantage. The plan was easy, simple, and clean. We were going to blast the Satans straight back to hell. And that's exactly what we did. Unfortunately, it was only temporary, because as you and I both know, they came back."

"How did they come back?" I asked.

"Funny thing about revenge. As you know, it's fueled by emotion. When emotion is involved, common sense seems to hide in the back corners of your mind. We thought we had destroyed their club. But we didn't get them all. A few members survived, bided their time, and recruited new members. A few years later, they reemerged."

"Oh. I guess that makes sense." He nodded and then I asked, "I know that my knowledge of the MC life is very minimal, but why did everyone stand behind Ice, knowing that he took action without consulting the rest of the club? I thought that was a big no-no in the MC world."

"Good question. I think we all could understand Ice's rage. Ace was very special to him. We all knew about him losing his parents and the history behind that. We all knew where he came from. Ace had given him something that he needed: a father." He paused for a moment and then added, "I know, it makes us sound like a bunch of pussies. But what Ice proved to the entire club that day was that his loyalty ran deep. We all knew that if anything like what happened to Ace happened to any other brother, Ice would avenge them with everything he had, even if it meant losing his own life. We were his family and he would protect anyone associated with

AMY CECIL

this club with his last breath. That kind of fierce loyalty is hard to find and we seek it out every day. Without loyalty like that, a club won't survive."

Just then, Ryder and Spike walked into the kitchen. Hawk asked, "Find anything?"

Ryder replied sarcastically, "You mean besides the dead body in the basement?" He laughed at his own wit, but Hawk was not amused at all.

"Very funny, asshole. You know what the fuck I'm talking about."

"Yeah, we found some clippings and shit in the office."

"What type of clippings?" Hawk asked.

"Creepy shit, Hawk. All kinds of stuff about Ice." He looked over at me apologetically and then continued, "You want us to take it to Betty's?"

Hawk asked, "You bring the van?" Ryder nodded. "Yeah, take it all. Then I want you to go see Reaper, see if he is burning anyone tomorrow. Get Grayson added to the lot. Wait until dark before you take the body out, then burn this place to the ground. Keep this contained, you got me?"

"You got it, boss. We'll be back to get this shithole cleaned up tonight," Ryder replied. They left without another word. I felt like I had been dropped inside an episode of *Sons of Anarchy* and that none of this was real. But it was real. Grayson's dead body in the basement was very real. *Is this my life now?*

After Ryder and Spike left, I asked Hawk the one question that had been plaguing me since we discovered Mark's body. "So, with this new discovery, do you think Caden is alive?"

Hawk hesitated for a moment, then said, "Yes, darl'n, it's looking that way."

"Well, what are we waiting for? We need to find him!"

"No, Emma, we don't. He is staying away for a reason. Ice knows what he is doing. He'll make contact when necessary and he'll come back when the time is right. It appears that he wants to remain dead for a reason. I'm not sure what that reason is, but if I had to guess, I'd say it has something to do with protecting you and the club." He waited, letting what he said sink in, and then

58

continued, "We need to keep up the pretense that he is dead. Do you ladies understand what I mean by that?"

"I think," I said. Honey nodded.

"Well, just to make sure we are all on the same page: Emma, you play the part of the grieving widow. Honey, you just lost your best friend. You got me?"

Honey and I both agreed.

"Can you both handle that?" It was not going to be easy, but I trusted Hawk. I didn't know why—after all, I hardly knew him—but from what I had seen from him in the last several hours, I believed that Caden trusted him. Therefore, I trusted him.

He got up from the table and headed to the back rooms. I assumed he was checking with Dbag and Doc to see what they found. Thinking about all that they were going through, I was thankful that I wasn't in their shoes. Honey and I just sat at the table and waited. I had no words. Everything Hawk had told me and everything that I had seen today was slowly consuming my thoughts.

Twenty minutes later Hawk returned to the kitchen. "Come on, ladies, let's get you both home. The boys have things under control here." We got up to leave. Hawk drove us back to his bike. Before he and Honey left he gave me a piece of paper with some phone numbers on it. "If you need us for anything, Emma, you call me. If you remember anything else, call." I nodded and got into the driver's seat. They left and I drove back to my apartment.

As I approached my apartment door, I could see a bouquet of flowers lying at my door. As I got closer, I could see that they had not come from a florist. They were handpicked wildflowers wrapped together with a bow. Pinned to one of the stems was a note:

I hear you say my name
I never left you
I'm everywhere
I kiss your cheek with the wind
I embrace you with the sun
Can you feel our love

Do you know I'm already there[i]

The note wasn't signed, but I knew. Caden was indeed alive. This was his way of telling me not to worry about him. Like Hawk said, he was staying away for a reason. I knew he would resurface when the time was right.

CHAPTER 8

Rebel

I had about five miles to go before I reached Ari's school by the time I had hung up with Ice. I thought back to our conversation. Had he really just given me his blessing to date his sister? Did I really hear him right? All this time, I had been avoiding a relationship with Ari because I thought Ice would kill me, when really, if I would have just asked him, Ari and I could have been together long ago. I sighed and shook my head. Now was not the time to worry about that. I'd let Ice get this mess straightened out first; I just needed to get Ari home and keep her and Emma safe.

I pulled up to her apartment; I knew she would be home. I'd had her most current class schedule each semester since she started college three years ago. When I knocked, I heard her say, "Coming." It'd been almost six months since I last saw her, and I wondered if she had changed at all. Just then, she opened the door. She was still as beautiful as ever. "Fire!" she exclaimed. "What are you doing here?" she asked, looking around. I assumed she was looking for her brother or any other members of the club.

"Hey, girl! Aren't you going to ask me in?" I asked.

"Oh gosh, I'm so sorry. You just surprised me! Come in!"

After I got inside and she closed the door, she ran into my arms and gave me a big hug. *Damn, I've missed her.*

She said, "So why are you here? Is everything ok? Caden?"

"Everyone is fine. But I need to bring you back to Edinboro. We need to leave today."

"Why, what happened?" she asked.

"I'll tell you what: why don't you get some things packed, we'll go get something to eat before we get on the road, and I'll tell you everything. How's that?" She looked at me curiously. She knew there was something that I wasn't telling her. But like a good girl, she went back into her bedroom and 30 minutes later, she came out with two suitcases.

"Uh, sweetheart, that ain't gonna work," I said.

"What?" she asked, confused.

"Darl'n, I've just got my bike. I can't take all that shit." The look on her face was priceless. I couldn't help but start laughing at her.

"Fire, stop it! Quit laughing at me!" she yelled.

Shit, she's mad at me. I walked over to her and pulled her in close. We were nose to nose and I could feel her sweet breath on my face. We were so close that I could have kissed her if I wanted to. Hell, I did want to, but that was for a later time. I could tell by the look in her eyes that she wanted it too. I had to step away, and her look of desire changed to one of disappointment. I said, "I'm not laughing at you. Not really. You're just cute, packing your entire life to go home when I am sure you have more than enough clothes and girly things there that you will forget about everything that is in that suitcase." I paused and then added, "And don't call me Fire!"

"But you told me to pack! And Fire's your name."

"No, it's not my name. My name is Balefire, but you know I prefer to be called Rebel. That's the name your brother gave me the day I met him and it's the name I prefer. And when I told you to pack, I was thinking you'd only take a few things that you absolutely can't live without. All I got is two saddlebags on my bike, babe, so I really mean a few things. Not your whole fucking closet and bathroom."

She seemed to calm down, but I could tell she still was not happy. She laid each suitcase down on its side and opened them up. She grabbed her Kindle, her laptop, a bunch of chargers, and a rather large makeup bag. She laid those items on the bed, zipped up the suitcases, and dragged them back to her bedroom. I should have helped her, but I was just a little shocked at what I'd just witnessed. The items that she could not live without were all electronic, except for the makeup bag. I'd expected her to grab a shit-pile of makeup and clothes. Go figure.

She came back out of the bedroom and asked as she gestured toward the items on the bed, "Do you have room for this stuff?"

I smiled. "I sure do. There is probably a little bit more room if there is anything else that you want to take."

She looked around the room and then turned and walked back to her bedroom. A few seconds later, she came back with a picture frame and a teddy bear. I couldn't help but smile. I recognized both items. I'd given them both to her on her birthday last year. Inside the picture frame was a picture of the two of us.

"Ready?" I asked.

"Yep, let's go. There is a great place in town to eat. We can go there. Okay?"

"Lead the way, princess!"

After I got her stuff safely stowed, I got on my bike. I turned back toward her and said, "Your turn." She loved riding, and I loved having her on the back of my bike. As she slowly lifted her leg over my bike to get on, she leaned her body into mine. I could smell her perfume as she pressed snugly up against me. She knew exactly what she was doing and I could feel my dick getting hard. *Damn woman, I swear she does that shit just to get a rise out of me ... literally.* I revved the bike and off we went.

She directed me through town to the Garryowen Irish Pub. I'd heard good things about this place and was looking forward to trying it. I parked the bike and locked it up, and then we headed into the pub. Once we were seated and had ordered our food and drinks, she asked, "Ok, Reb, what's going on?"

I told her everything. I told her about Emma coming back. I explained to her that Emma's friend needed the help of the club and that the Satans had her. I told her about Mark Grayson and the clubhouse being bombed. I had to assure her several times that nobody was hurt. She asked, "Ok, so what aren't you telling me?"

I realized I still had not told her about Ice. "Well, there is more." I didn't know where to go. It was like there was a block in my brain. I was just having a hard time asking her to pretend that her brother was dead.

"Rebel, Ice sent you here for a reason. Get to the point. I'm not a kid anymore and I can handle the truth, whatever it is."

She was right about that, she sure as hell wasn't a kid anymore. "So, it turns out that this Mark Grayson guy is your half-brother." I didn't know how else to tell her except to just come straight out with it.

"Are you crazy? Caden is my only brother."

I explained to her the connection. I told her that her dad was not Ice's dad. I told her about Ace. I told her everything.

"So, I have another brother, big deal," she said nonchalantly.

"Well, sweetheart, there's more. Grayson is the one that had the clubhouse blown up. He tried to kill Ice. But Ice beat him at his own game and killed him. He's dead."

"Okay, what else?"

"This is where it gets a little tricky. Your brother wants the Satans—and the majority of the club—to believe he is dead," I said, as delicately as I could.

"That's ridiculous. Why would he want that?"

"Actually, he is doing it for a very good reason. You see, Grayson had big ties to the Satans. If the Satans find out that Ice killed him, they'll come after him, Emma, the club, and even you. They will go after everything that he loves. He's lying low so that he can broker a peace between the two clubs. No more biker war and no more worrying about our families."

"I still don't fully understand. But I trust my brother. He's doing what he needs to do, I guess." She thought a moment and asked, "Why do I have to go home?"

"Well, you and I are the only ones that know for sure that Ice is alive. After today, I'm guessing that Hawk, Emma, and Honey believe that he is alive. And if they do what Ice is expecting them to do, they are going to just let everyone else believe he is dead. I will talk to Hawk when I get back so he knows for sure."

"So where do I come in? I still don't understand why I have to go home. It's my senior year, Rebel. I'm about to graduate from college. If I leave for any extended amount of time, I won't graduate."

"Your brother understands that and he will figure things out for you. You know he won't let you down. But right now, he needs your help. If we want everyone to believe that he is dead, but you don't come home for any type of service, that would look odd. You need to play the part and mourn him with everyone else. Can you do that?"

She thought for a moment, then said, "Yes, I can. I would do anything for my brother." She paused for a moment, then added, "Take me home, Reb."

I motioned for the waitress to bring us our check, paid the bill, and we left. Five minutes later, we were on my bike heading to Edinboro. I was in heaven. I had hours ahead of me with this incredible woman on the back of my bike, her arms around me. One of these days, she was going to be my old lady. Hell, Ice had even said it was ok. Hadn't he?

Four and a half hours later, we were pulling up to Betty's Dinor. I had phoned Hawk while we were on the road and told him that I was heading back and that I needed to speak with him. He told me to meet him at Betty's. After I parked the bike out front, we went inside.

"Why are we here? I thought you were taking me home," Ari said.

"I am, but I need to talk to Hawk first. Why don't you get yourself something to eat or drink? I'll be back down in a few minutes. This won't take long."

"Ok. Don't be too long, I'm tired."

She's tired? I've been on that bike for over eight hours today. I mean shit, I love my bike, but it's been a long day for me as well.

I headed to the back of the diner and went up the back steps. I walked into a rather large room with a table in the center. Hawk was sitting at the table. There were four other doors off to the side, but all in all, it was a really small space compared to what we'd had at the clubhouse. "You got Ari?" Hawk asked.

"Yep, she's downstairs waiting. Do you have a minute to talk?" I asked.

"Sure, things are quiet right now. It's been a busy and informative day."

"Tell me about it," I said.

"So, what's up?"

"Ice is alive." I didn't know how else to say it except to just put it out there.

He didn't look too surprised. Ice had said that he would probably have figured things out by now, and apparently he had.

"I figured as much. You've talked to him?"

"Yeah, he called me right after he killed Grayson." Hawk looked a little slighted and I felt that I needed to justify Ice's actions. "I think he called me first because he knew that you would have so many things to take care of after the explosion and his disappearance. He needed me to get Ari, and he knew that as soon as you found Grayson, you would know he was alive. He's been watching you all, so he knew that you guys did indeed find Grayson. You get all that, right?"

Hawk's demeanor softened a bit—it looked like he was starting to see the big picture. None of us had time right now for hurt feelings. "Yeah, I get it. So what's his plan?"

"Well, he wants me to take Ari, Emma, and Honey to his house on the lake. He believes that they will be safe there until he can get things figured out."

"Figured out? Is he winging this?" Hawk asked, irritated.

"No, he has a plan. He just needs us to keep up the pretense that he is dead. He knows that you and the girls know he's alive, but everyone else needs to believe he is dead—especially the Satans. If they think he is dead, then they will not know if he killed Grayson or if Grayson killed him. They will hold back on their retaliation until that is confirmed. That buys him time to work on brokering a peace between the two clubs. That's his plan."

"So he wants a wake and he wants peace?" Hawk asked.

"Yeah, I believe so. We are all tired of this feud between the clubs. Aren't you?"

"I am," he said, sounding tired. Then he added with a laugh, "I will be happy when we get back to the days of being Harley enthusiasts!"

"Me too, but there's more."

"More?"

"He knows why Mark did all this. Brianne, Emma, all of it."

"I figured it was because Ice took his woman."

"No. It goes much deeper than that. Brace yourself." I paused for a moment, then continued, "Mark Grayson is Ace's son. So is Ice." I waited for him to let that information sink in.

"What? Who told you this?"

"Ice did. Can you believe that?" I paused again, then added, "Ace had Grayson first. His mom abandoned him and left him with Ace. Ace gave him up for adoption because he felt that his MC life wasn't a good life for his kid. Later, Ace had an affair with Ice's mom before she got married. When she got pregnant, he told her to raise the kid on her own. Told her that the MC life wasn't a place to raise a kid. She married Tyler Jackson and everyone believed that Ice was Tyler's kid. Ice joining the club after his parents died was all by chance. And I guess when Ace figured out who he was, he felt there was no harm since he was all grown up and he had just lost his parents. When Grayson found out, he got pissed 'cause he felt that Ice stole the life that was meant for him. So for years now, he'd been planning his revenge on his brother. Taking Brianne was part of it as well. She found out who he was and was going to tell Emma. He had to silence her, and the only way he knew how without just killing her was to get the Satans involved."

"Holy shit. That's fucked up. You know, Emma mentioned Brianne when she told me about Grayson abducting her. I wonder if she is still alive. Emma seemed to think so ... but I'm sure they've probably fucked her up so much, that poor girl."

"I think Ice is working on that as well. I think he will do what he can to get her home safe. He promised Emma, and for as long as I've known him, he's never broken his promises."

"You got that right. Wow, that's a lot to take in. I just can't believe that Ace knew Ice was his kid. But I guess if he told Ace who his parents were, Ace had to have known." He shook his head, and then added, "Just mind-blowing."

"I know. But Ice is one strong motherfucker. He can handle this."

"Yeah. If anyone can, he can." He paused for a moment then continued, "So, I'll call Emma and let her know that you will be coming to get her. I will go get Honey and bring her to the lake house. Oh, and I don't want Ari at the house alone when you go and get Emma. I'll call Spike to meet you over there and he can stay with Ari until you get there. I'd send him to get Emma, but I think she would feel better with you. Sound good?"

"Are you sure he can handle Ari? I want her safe, Hawk!" I said.

"Spike will be fine for the hour or so that you are not there. You do not need to worry about Ari, she will be safe," he replied.

"Fine," I grumbled. "Talk to you later."

"Once everyone is safe at Ice's house, you know what you need to do. Ice, this club, and those girls are all counting on you."

"You got it, Hawk! Consider it done." Between Ice, Hawk, and me, those girls were very special to us. Hawk had never mentioned it, but I knew he'd always had a thing for Honey. I guessed he gave up when she and Ice hooked up. But now that Ice was off the market, Honey was fair game. *Fuck, we sound like a bunch of soap opera characters. I guess even the toughest of guys have chick problems.*

I went back downstairs to gather Ari and a few minutes later, we were back on the road.

CHAPTER 9

Emma

"I've been telling you all along that Caden was alive. I knew it! Thank you for calling," I said to Hawk through the phone.

"Wait, Emma, there's more," Hawk said.

"He's ok, isn't he?" I asked, afraid of the answer.

"He's fine. Really. But he doesn't want you staying in that apartment anymore. He wants you to stay at his house with Ari and Honey."

His house? I didn't know Caden had a house. I thought he just lived at the clubhouse. But now that I think about it, where would Ari stay when she was home from school? I guess he would need a place for her.

"Hawk, I am fine here. I don't think there is anything to worry about now that Mark is dead."

"Emma, please. Don't fight me on this. This is what Ice wants. You know as well as I do that when he wants something done, it gets done. Don't make it difficult for us. You know that if you don't go quietly, we'll come and carry you off. And it won't be pretty." He was right about that. I looked around my apartment. I was living alone, and it would be nice to see Ari again. Hawk continued, "Why don't you get some bags packed? Rebel will be by in about a half hour to get you. He will have his bike, so leave your bags in the living room and the door unlocked when you leave. I will send one of the guys with a cage to collect them for you. I think you should plan on staying at Ice's indefinitely. You know that once he gets back, you most likely will not be leaving." He chuckled into the phone. I found it endearing to see how his attitude had changed now that he knew Ice was alive.

He was probably right, too. And in actuality, I wanted it that way. I'd missed Caden so much over the last week. "Ok Hawk, tell Rebel I will be ready."

"Good girl! Talk to you soon."

After Hawk hung up the phone, I looked around the apartment again. *What do I need to pack?* I went to the closet and grabbed a suitcase. I spent ten minutes rummaging through my clothes, grabbing as much as I could fit in the suitcase. I knew that once Caden got back, we would get everything else moved. I then took a smaller suitcase into the bathroom and just dumped everything in there. Twenty minutes later, I was ready to go. I looked around the apartment for anything else that I might need. I had already packed my laptop. I looked in the refrigerator. It had been so long since I had been home, it smelled like a trash can in there. I got a trash bag and dumped everything from the refrigerator in there. There wasn't much, but it had all spoiled and needed to go.

Ten minutes later, Rebel was knocking on my door.

The drive to Caden's house was long and curvy and very secluded. As we approached the end of his driveway, it appeared that we were looking at the back of the house. I assumed the front faced the lake. There was a two-stall garage, and there were very few windows on the back. Rebel parked the bike and we walked around to the front of the house. As the front of the house came into view, I realized why I hadn't seen many windows before. They were all in the front. The house was absolutely gorgeous. It was a cedar and stone two-story mansion. The house had three balconies with stone pillars going down to the main level. The entire right corner of the house was all windows with an incredible view of the lake. Toward the center of the house was the main balcony, opening into a huge great room that spanned the entire height of the house. To the right of the house was a stone walkway that led to a breezeway underneath the balconies that led to the door. This wasn't a house, it was a freakin' hotel. I hadn't even seen the inside yet and I already loved it.

When we got inside, I was even more amazed. A large great room encompassed the downstairs, with vaulted ceilings, a huge kitchen with a bar off to the right, and a game room with a pool table to the left of the kitchen. The surface of the pool table had a TV screen built into it. It was unlike anything I had ever seen. The living room part of the great room had a huge, floor-to-ceiling stone fireplace, and there was a smaller fireplace in the game room. On the other side of the living room was a small staircase that only went up partially. I realized then that the house was not a two-story home, but a three-story home. This house was totally unbelievable. *Where did Caden get all this money?* I thought to myself. This house was easily a million-dollar home. Obviously the MC life had been good to him. The small partial staircase led upstairs to three bedrooms, each with their own bathroom. Off to the right of the kitchen was another staircase that led to the third floor.

It appeared that nobody was home, which I thought was odd because Hawk had told me that Rebel was dropping Ari off first before he came to get me. Then, like a hurricane, Ari came running down the small staircase.

"Emma!" she cried. She ran right to me and hugged me. "It's so good to see you! It's been so long!"

"Ari, my goodness, look at you. You've grown into a beautiful young lady!" I couldn't believe it, she was all grown up and stunning.

"Oh, Emma, I've missed you so much!" she said.

"I've missed you, too."

As she grabbed my hand and encouraged me to walk with her, she said, "Come on, let me show you around." She walked me around the house showing me all around the great room, the second-floor bedrooms, and the kitchen. Even with Ari here, I was still having a hard time believing this was Caden's home. I'd always gotten the impression that he lived at the clubhouse.

She then took me up the stairs to the third floor. It was all one big bedroom. It was fantastic, and it was clear that this was Cade's room. "I assume you will be sleeping here," she said as she winked at me. "And, I might add, it's about time you two worked through your shit." Well, I couldn't disagree with her on that. She leaned over the railing and called down to Rebel and Spike as they were bringing my bags in. "You guys can put Emma's things up here, please." They headed to the stairs. She turned to me and said, "I'll let you get settled. Honey will be here shortly and hopefully, she will fix us some dinner."

"I can fix something if you are hungry," I said.

Ari smiled. "Let's have Honey do it tonight. That will give us a chance to catch up."

I agreed. It really was great seeing Ari again. It had been so long.

After the boys and Ari left, I walked around Caden's room. He had a massive king-size bed with two end tables on each side. There was an armoire in the room, along with a huge walk-in closet. His clothes only filled up a quarter of the closet. There were also two built-in dressers in the closet. I opened the drawers and found them empty. At least there was a place for my clothes. I hoped there would be room for me in the bathroom as well.

I walked into the adjoining bathroom. It was bigger than the bedroom at my apartment. I had no worries about space in this bathroom. There was more than enough space in here for both Caden and me, as well as a football team or two. The shower was all in teak wood and completely open with four different showerheads coming through at different angles. There were all kinds of switches on the wall, with no indication as to what they controlled. I made a mental note to ask Ari about that.

Once I got everything settled, I headed back downstairs. The smell coming from the kitchen was intoxicating, letting me know that Honey had arrived. I'd always been proud of my cooking, but she was phenomenal.

I walked into the kitchen and greeted Honey. "Hey, Honey. That smells amazing. What'cha making?" I asked.

"Hey, Emma. Chicken Marsala—you are smelling the wine. It makes the whole meal," she replied.

"I wasn't hungry, but now that I smell that, suddenly I'm starved. You are a fantastic cook."

"Thank you. I don't know about being fantastic, but I do enjoy it." She paused for a brief moment, then added, "So what do you think about all this? It's like a slumber party of some sort." She smirked, then added, "I'm too old for slumber parties."

I laughed. "Aren't we all? But I look at it this way: Cade is doing everything he can to keep the ones he loves most safe. I'm just thankful that he is still alive."

"Yeah, me too."

Just then Ari came to join us. We sat at the bar and watched Honey work her magic. We offered several times to help her, but she refused. She insisted that she did best when she worked alone, so Ari and I didn't argue.

I noticed that she was making quite a lot of food—definitely more than the three of us could eat. "Honey, why are you making so much?"

"I need to feed the boys, too."

"Boys?"

"Yeah, Hawk, Spike, and Rebel stayed. Once they heard I was cooking, they weren't leaving. I think they are already sick of eating at the diner." She laughed, and then added, "They are out back sitting by the lake. I think Rebel is going to stay with us, just in case."

"Just in case?" I asked curiously.

"Yeah, they want to make sure one of the guys is with us at all times. No worries, they are just looking out for our safety," she said reassuringly.

"Oh. I see. Do you really think we are in danger?"

Ari chimed in and said, "If my brother believes we are, then we are. His instincts are right on, and I would never question something that he feels in his gut."

Honey added, "She's got that right."

They knew him so much better than I did, and I was the one that knew him the longest. Somehow, I needed to fix that. *Just wait until you get home, Caden Jackson*, I thought to myself.

After dinner, we spent the remainder of the night chatting. Hawk and Spike left not long after we finished with the dinner dishes. Rebel stayed, but he plopped himself down onto the recliner on the opposite side of the room. It seemed like he wanted to let us girls have some time together. I noticed on several occasions he kept looking over at Ari—not just looking, but staring. It kinda weirded me out at first, but knowing Rebel like I did—and I knew him better that I knew most of the other club members—I realized it wasn't weird at all. Rebel was in love with Ari. *So that is the girl he was talking about. Gee, I wonder how Caden feels about that.*

At one point while we girls were gabbing away, Rebel's phone rang. He spoke in a hushed tone and I could not make out what he was saying. He was only on the phone for a minute or so, then he hung up and put his phone away. When he didn't say anything to us about his phone call, I let it go. It was probably about club business that we ladies were not privy to.

When we were all talked out, we decided to call it a night. I headed upstairs while Honey and Ari went to the downstairs bedrooms. Rebel was still sitting in the living room. I turned back and asked him, "Aren't you going to bed?"

"Naw, not yet. I got a couple of things to do first. Don't worry about me, Emma dear. It's all good. Sweet dreams," he said.

"Ok, if you say so. Goodnight, Rebel." I was tired, it had been a long and exhausting day and that bed upstairs was calling my name.

CHAPTER 10

Caden

I waited patiently for Rebel to come out back to get me. Well, patiently was not the right word. I wasn't patient at all. I was anxious to see my girl. I'd called him about an hour ago and told him that I wanted to come into the house once the girls had gone to bed. It was best that I didn't just walk into my house immediately, just in case I was being watched.

"It's about time. What the hell took so long?" I asked as he came out onto the deck.

"Sorry boss, they were up talking. You know how girls are when they get together, it turns into an all-night gab session," he said apologetically.

"I know, I know." I paused briefly then added, "So, did they all go to bed?"

"Yeah, about a half hour ago. I wanted to make sure that Ari and Honey were asleep before I let you in," Rebel said.

"Good thinking. I'm not ready to reunite with everyone just yet. I still need to stay away. Hell, I know I shouldn't be here. But I've been so worried about Emma...I just need to see her."

"Ice, man, nobody could blame you for that. I totally get it. Come on, get inside before someone sees you. 'Course, I really don't think anyone of interest knows that this is your house."

He had a point there. I'd worked very hard to keep this house off the radar. I wanted a place for Ari in which she would feel safe. I wanted her to know that she always had a home. Even though I preferred to stay at our old clubhouse, it had never been her home. This place was and would always be her home. And, if everything went as planned, it would soon be Emma's home too.

I walked into the house and straight up to the loft, taking the steps two at a time. As I rushed upstairs I could hear Rebel downstairs, quietly saying, "You're welcome. Have a good night." He snickered.

Little fucker. I didn't even thank him.

I walked down the hallway and quietly stepped into the archway of my room. The room was dark and moonlight shined through the window. It silhouetted Emma's body as she lay on her side, facing away from me. Making as little noise as possible, I walked toward the bed. I could tell by her breathing that she was already asleep. I thought, *I should let her sleep. She has had a rough day.* I stood there for a few minutes just watching her. I couldn't take my eyes off of her. She was so beautiful.

After about 15 minutes of just watching my baby sleep, I turned to leave. I didn't have the heart to wake her and figured it was probably best that I left her alone—for now. But as I started to leave the bedroom, I heard a whisper. "Cade? Is that you?" I stopped and waited. Then she asked again, "Cade?" She was silent for a brief moment, then she spoke again, "Please don't go." That was it; there was no way I could leave her after that.

I turned back toward the bed. Her back was still away from me and for a second I thought that perhaps she was dreaming and talking in her sleep. I wanted her to be awake so bad that I couldn't help myself, and I answered her by saying, "Hey, beautiful."

She turned to face me, lying on her other side. I could barely make out the very pleased look on her face in the moonlight. She was fucking perfect and she was all mine. I could feel my jeans getting tighter as my dick got hard just looking at her. She reached down to the covers and moved them aside, inviting me to join her.

"How did you know I was here?" I asked her curiously.

"I could smell you," she whispered.

"That bad, baby? Sorry."

"Oh no. Not bad at all. You smell of leather and aftershave. You smell amazing. It's sexy," she said, clarifying her last remark.

"So now I smell sexy?" I sat down on the bed next to her and brushed the hair away from her face. "You're beautiful, baby. You know that?"

She smiled, then said, "So, are you just gonna sit here and tell me how beautiful I am, or are you gonna show me how much you missed me?"

With her words, I got up from the bed and began removing my clothes, my eyes never leaving hers as she watched me intently. When I was fully undressed I crawled into bed next to her. Her body was soft and warm and for the first time in this house and in this bed, I truly felt that I was home. As I pulled her into my arms, I realized at that moment that everything I had was hers. Everything that I did from that moment on would be for her.

"God I've missed you," I said as she nuzzled into my neck.

"I'm still waiting, Cade," she stated.

"Waiting?" I asked curiously.

"Really? Do I have to spell it out for you?" She slowly ran her hand down the length of my naked body and suddenly my dick realized what she was talking about. It didn't take my brain long to figure out what she meant.

"Who are you and what did you do with my shy, proper Emma?" I laughed.

She giggled. "Oh, baby ... she's still here. But you see, you have given her a taste of you and that incredibly sexy body of yours, and now, I'm afraid to say, she can't get enough of you."

Her words lit a fire in me and I had to have her. But before I could take control of the situation, she crawled up on top of me. Straddling me, she bent down and licked my bottom lip before devouring my mouth. Her tongue was warm and wet, and it only made me want her more. When she was done kissing me, she sat up and pulled her tank top over her head, exposing her bare chest. Her tits were perfect. I sat up, bringing her body closer to mine, which allowed me to suck on her nipples. She moaned, and then she demanded, "Harder, Ice. Harder!"

What. The. Fuck! Where did that come from? She called me Ice! I hadn't thought my dick could get any harder, but her words had proved me wrong. As my lady commanded, I sucked harder. She was in a trance, totally lost in the pleasure that I was giving her. I thought, *I bet if I had more time, I could make her come by just sucking on her tits. I'll have to remember that.*

At that point, however, I could not take any more and I needed to be in control. I rolled her off me and at the same time positioned myself on top of her. She was lying on the bed underneath me looking at me with so much hunger in her eyes. I felt so much love for her, I could no longer hold it back. She needed to know how I felt. I leaned down close to her and whispered in her ear, "I love you." I kissed her softly on her neck as my cock slid slowly into her sweet pussy. I moved as slowly as I could, because I wanted to savor that moment. I wanted to savor every inch as I pushed into her. We weren't fucking. It was no longer about getting laid or having to have her. We were doing something that I had never done before. We were making love.

She was so fucking tight, and her pussy clamped onto my dick like a vise. I felt as if I was going to explode. I had to stop, so I drew out of her slowly and then waited before I slid back in. Carefully, I pushed into her again, trying desperately to keep control of my movements. I continued this several times and I could have sworn she clenched my dick tighter each time. I was losing control, and I thought she was too.

"Tell me, Emma. Tell me what I need to hear."

Without hesitation or questioning, she responded, "I love you." I moved my fingers over her clit. She was soaking wet around my cock and my fingers. I was about to come, but I needed her to ride it out with me.

"Give it to me, sweetheart, give me all you got." With my words, she detonated beneath me and I watched her lose herself to me. Seeing her orgasm was my undoing, and I took my release with her as we rode out our passion together.

Afterwards, she was snuggled up against me, tracing the tat on my chest. She loved that dragon for some reason, I wasn't sure why.

"You're not staying, are you?" she asked quietly.

I didn't say anything for a minute, and then I replied, "No, baby, I can't."

She stopped tracing my tat and was silent for a while. Then she asked, "Why did you come back, then?"

"I would like to think that is obvious," I said.

"Oh, I see," she said. Suddenly I was reminded of Emma the little girl who didn't get what she wanted.

"What's the matter, princess? And don't tell me 'nothing'. I can hear it in your voice."

"Nothing," she said.

"What did I just say? I know something is wrong. Now tell me what the fuck is bothering you before I spank that perfect ass of yours." Her body snuggled up closer to me, but she was not getting out of this one. I added, "Don't go trying to get me to take you again. It's not working. Now tell me."

She looked up at me, knowing she had no choice but to tell me. "Well, earlier you said you loved me. But now, you say that the only reason you came back was to get laid."

"When did I say that was the only reason I came back?"

"You said it was obvious. Anyone could figure out what you meant by that from your actions this evening."

"Emma, baby, that's not what I meant. I meant I came back because I love you, sweetheart, and I just had to see you, to tell you how I feel. I realized earlier that I never really said it, and when Grayson took you, one of my worst nightmares was that something awful would happen to you and you would never know how I truly felt about you. Don't you understand, baby? You are my world now. We are spending the rest of our lives together. I am nothing without you."

I felt wetness on my chest and realized that she was crying. "Emma?" She was silent. "Baby, are you ok?" I asked again.

Muffled by her tears, she said, "Cade, did you just propose to me?"

I thought, *well, shit*. I hadn't realized it when I'd said it, but I guess I kinda had proposed. I knew I wanted to marry her and to spend the rest of my life with her. But I also wanted her proposal to be special ... not with me just stopping in for a night and then leaving her again for God knows how long.

"In a way, babe, yeah, I did. But this is not the official proposal. When I propose to you, baby, you will not question whether I am proposing or not. You will know, and damn it, woman, you fucking better say yes!"

She moved up to face me, her lips barely touching my own. "I'm saying yes now and I will say yes then. I love you, Caden." She kissed me with a soft, sweet kiss and lay back down to snuggle against me. Moments later we were sated, happy, and asleep.

CHAPTER 11

Emma

When I woke the next morning it was still dark outside. I glanced over at the clock on the end table; it read 4:12 am. I first thought, *why am I up so early?* Then I realized I could hardly breathe. Cade was practically laying on top of me. I thought, *why does he always do this?* His weight was pressing on my chest and I was suffocating. I had to get up. Carefully, trying not to disturb him, I wriggled away. The house was still quiet, so I assumed that nobody else was awake yet.

I stood there for a moment watching him sleep. He was so damn sexy. The covers had been tossed off the bed and he was laying there on his stomach, completely naked. He looked a little different from when I saw him last. His hair seemed longer and he had a beard, which was jet-black like his hair, but was also speckled with gray. I could stare at him all day. The club rocker tat on his back was incredible; this was the first time I had a chance to really look at it. *Knights of Silence* was tattooed in an arc at the top of the design. Underneath, in an arc curving in the opposite direction, was tattooed *Edinboro Chapter*. The words were cool and everything, but the most intriguing part of the tat was the design that filled the center section.

It was an odd design: a menacing dragon encompassing a Celtic cross. The wings of the dragon were open and hooded the entire image. The image was engulfed in flames. I wondered what it all meant. I knew a little about Celtic animal symbols, and I knew the dragon represented all of creation, symbolizing power and vitality. If I remembered correctly, it was considered the most powerful Celtic symbol. I could see that some of this tied to the MC, but I wasn't seeing the whole picture. Then I realized Caden's tat was identical to the image on the back of his cut, just not quite so detailed.

After inspecting his tat—along with his incredible body—I figured it'd be best if I got into the shower. I knew he'd be up soon and I guessed he would have to leave. *When will I see him again? I can't think about that now. I have a part to play today, and it has to be my best performance. Thank God it's just acting.*

I was just finishing my shower when I heard the bathroom door open. At first, I was startled, but then I remembered it was probably just Cade. There was no shower curtain to hide behind, so I soon saw him in all his delicious glory. *Ok*, I thought, *so perhaps he wasn't going to get up and leave right away.* By the look on his face, he definitely had other things in mind. He sauntered over to me and stood as close as he could get to me. Before I had time to think, he grabbed me and pulled me up against his body. Instinctively, I wrapped my legs and arms around him as he pushed me against the shower wall. He didn't say a word. Instead, he took my mouth in a rough and deep kiss. He'd never kissed me like that before and the sensation of his beard against my skin was intoxicating. There was so much need and passion in every movement of his mouth. His tongue thrusted into me over and over, and I felt his hardness pushing against me as he pumped his hips in time with his tongue. He had lit a fire in me, and I felt like a cat in heat.

His right hand slid down my back, cupping my ass. His strength was overwhelming and only made me want him more. With his right hand pinned between my ass and the shower wall, he took his left hand and reached under my thigh, continuing further right to my core. I was dripping wet, and not from the water that was pummeling down on me. His fingers entered me, sending me into shuttering convulsions, and I knew if he continued that I wasn't going to last. He pulled his mouth away from me and talked to me with his eyes, all while his fingers continued to fuck me. He was asking me if I wanted more. I was losing my mind, and all I could do was nod. Words had failed me. Then, he stopped. *What. The. Fuck.*

"Caden, please," I begged. He just grinned and began again. He worked me just to the point of orgasm over and over again, never allowing me any release. I couldn't take it anymore. I cried, "Cade, please, give it to me. Now!" Every nerve in my body was completely over stimulated. I needed a release, and I needed him to give it to me.

Before I knew what was happening, Caden let me go and turned me around so I was facing the wall. "Bend over and brace yourself on the wall," he directed. "This is gonna be hard and fast, baby."

I did as I was told and then said, "The harder the better." I think my words were his undoing. He entered me with a fury of lust, pounding into me. It felt like my insides were going to explode with pleasure. His hands reached around me, one cupping my breast, the other traveling down my belly to my clit. That was my undoing. I erupted into the most intense orgasm my body had ever known. My pussy continued to contract around him as I rode out my orgasm. The pulsating wouldn't stop, it was that intense—and then I felt a warm sensation run down my leg. Caden had found his release. Once he was done, he leaned over my body holding me close. "God, baby, I fucking love you!" he whispered.

He gave me a chaste kiss on my back and stepped away. My legs felt like rubber bands, and I didn't think I could move without falling over. I just stayed where I was, still holding onto the shower wall for support.

"Babe?" he asked. "Are you ok?"

I couldn't do anything but nod.

He came around and squatted down to face me, saying, "Oh, baby, did I hurt you?"

If he only knew. I looked at him with all the love in my eyes as I started to stand up. He stood too and grabbed my hand to give me support. I was feeling very light-headed and I needed to get my wits about me before I spoke. I could see the worry in his expression and I was doing everything I could to ease his mind.

As I started to feel better, I reached up and touched the side of his face. "No, baby, you didn't hurt me." Relief washed over his face. He really believed that he had hurt me. Poor baby. I added, "You just gave me the best fuck I have ever had." He grinned, obviously pretty proud of himself.

"Emma, my love, you got that all wrong. You just gave me the best fuck of my life," he said as he pulled me into his arms.

I had never felt such happiness as I did at that moment. And then, I suddenly remembered Mark and what had been done to him. How could a man who had so much love and care in his heart do that? I knew I was going to be sorry for asking, because deep down, I already knew the answer ... but I still had to ask.

I waited until we got out of the shower. We were back in the bedroom getting dressed when I asked, "Caden, did you kill Mark?" I couldn't hold it in any longer; I just had to know. As happy as I was to have him here—even knowing that he would be gone again sooner than I wanted—I still could not get the image of Mark's body out of my head.

He was silent.

I asked again. "Caden, I saw Mark at the house. I saw what was done to him. So please, tell me. I need to know. Did you do that to him?"

By the way he was acting, I knew the answer. Hawk had said he did it. Now he'd confirmed it. "Yes," he replied, in almost a whisper.

"Why? You didn't just kill him, Cade, you tortured him. You mutilated his body and hung him like a side of beef in a meat locker awaiting a butcher. How could you do such a thing?"

"Emma, I was in the house with you. I was bound and gagged in that basement and he had cameras on you. He made me watch everything, even when he tried to rape you. I did everything in my power to get free, but at first my anger got the best of me and I couldn't concentrate enough to free myself. When he left you alone, I was able to relax a little and I was finally able to get free. I couldn't act immediately because I had to wait until I knew you were safe. I didn't know what I would encounter if I went upstairs, and I wasn't about to take any chances with the one shot I had. I couldn't risk your life. So I waited and bided my time. When he told you to leave, I knew my time had come. All the anger that was in me from watching him touch you the way he did let loose. What you saw in the basement was the result of that anger."

To a point, I could understand his actions. At least, my heart did. My head was seeing something different; all it could see was a cold-blooded killer. He scared me. I asked, "Do you know why he did this? He gave me some information about Brianne telling me everything about him, but he never elaborated."

"Yes, I do," he replied.

"Well? Why, Caden?"

"It's a long story. I promise when this is all over, I will explain. I just can't right now; I really don't have a lot of time. I need to leave before the sun comes up."

"Can I ask one more question?"

"Sure, but it has to be quick. I've already spent too much time here."

"Is Brianne alive?" It was one answer I was dreading. I prayed that she was, but after all I had been through, I doubted it.

"I believe so, but I am not sure. When this is all said and done, I am hoping that when I come home, Brianne will be coming with me. Just trust me on this, please."

I decided to leave it at that. It was the best I could hope for under the circumstances. "Ok, I trust you." I was worried about the monster inside, but I still loved this man with every fiber of my being. He'd never let me down before. So, when I said that I trusted him, I really meant it.

Knowing that Caden would be leaving soon, I was already starting to sink into a little depression. I heard someone downstairs and peeked over the loft. It was Rebel, making coffee in the kitchen. Ari and Honey must still have been asleep. I turned to Caden, who was just putting on his shoes, and asked, "You're leaving now, aren't you?"

I could tell by the look on his face that he was just as bummed as I was. "Yeah, babe. The sooner I get this done, the sooner I can come home for good," he said.

I was quiet for a moment as I watched him lace up his boots, then I asked, "Caden, is there a chance that you might not come home?" I was worried. I was so afraid that this might be the last time I would ever see him.

He stopped messing with his boots and looked up at me. "Emma, nothing in life is for certain. I could have a normal job and this could be a normal day. I could be getting ready to go to work, let's say in a bank. I get dressed, I kiss my wife goodbye, and I leave. As I'm crossing the street, I get hit by a car and die. This is no different, sweetheart. We live every day never knowing for sure that the ones we love will return to us. The only thing that gets us through all that uncertainty is faith." He walked over to me and kissed me on the top of my head and continued, "Have faith, darl'n. Trust me, and I promise you I will do everything in my power to come back to you. You can count on that."

Tears welled up in my eyes as he pulled me into his arms. It was the best place in the world to be and I never wanted to let go. But I had to. He held me for a few minutes, then said, "I better go. I need to get out of here before the whole damn house wakes up." He walked over to loft railing and nodded to Rebel. He kissed me, and then he was gone.

After Caden left I walked over to the bed, sat down, and cried. I missed him already. A few minutes went by and I realized that crying over his leaving was not helping matters. I had to play the grieving widow later today; I'd save my crying for then. As I got up I glanced over at the nightstand. There was a slip of paper there with my name on it. I reached over to grab it and opened it. It said:

I'd give anything to hold you close
To touch your hair, to kiss your lips
When you think of me and the mistakes I've made
Try to understand that I am just a man.
The man who will love you until the end of time.[ii]

86

It wasn't signed. I guessed he hadn't wanted to leave any evidence. A lone tear escaped my eye and ran down my cheek. In that moment, it didn't matter who he'd killed. It didn't matter how he'd killed Mark. All that mattered was that I loved him and that I would always love him, no matter what. I prayed for his safe return.

Caden

Leaving Emma was one of the hardest things I'd ever had to do. I should have known better. I'd known seeing her last night was going to make it worse for both of us, but despite what my head was saying, my heart wasn't hearing it. It was just another bed I'd made that I had to lie in. The only good thing about all of this was that it would push me to get done what I needed to get done.

Unfortunately, I really couldn't do anything until after the club had my service. I wondered where they were with all of that. I needed to check in with Rebel later and find out. Now that Hawk was aware that Rebel knew, Hawk could keep Rebel informed. I only wanted one point of contact, it was cleaner that way.

So, for now, I just needed to lay low and watch the Satans.

CHAPTER 12

Rebel

Ice came downstairs, grabbed some coffee, and headed toward the door. "Thanks, man. Take care of our girls," he said as he approached the door.

"Sure thing, boss," I replied. Laughing to myself, I added, "Hey man, have fun driving that cage."

"Fuck you, Rebel! I'll be in touch." With those words, he was out the door. My president was always a ray of sunshine. But there wasn't any other person that I trusted to keep the club whole.

A few minutes after Ice left, Emma came downstairs. I could tell she had been crying and thought perhaps she needed some cheering up. "Good morning, Rebel," Emma said. "Did you sleep well?" she asked.

"I sure did. Did you sleep well?" I asked her teasingly, betting she hadn't gotten much sleep at all. She blushed—I knew that would get her.

"You just never mind how I slept, or I'm gonna tell on you!"

"Who you gonna tell?" I asked, baiting her.

Smugly, she replied, "I'm gonna tell my big badass biker old man—who, I might add, happens to be your president. That's who!"

I laughed. "Look at you, already playing the old lady card. Good girl, you learn quick," I replied. Then I added, "Don't forget that, either. There may come a day when you will need to play that card." She smiled and walked over to the coffee pot, poured herself some coffee, got some cream from the fridge, and then walked over to the bar and plopped herself onto a stool. That girl always put more cream in her coffee than actual coffee. It was disgusting.

"Are the girls up yet?"

I shook my head. "Naw, this is way too fuckin' early for Ari. That girl will sleep until noon if you let her. Honey will most likely be up in about an hour." I looked at my watch. "Her rise-and-shine time is usually 7 am."

"Wow, you know a lot about those two," she said, sounding surprised.

"What can I say? I know things."

We sat there in silence for a while. I was checking out the sports page of the paper and Emma was just sitting and staring off into space. After several minutes, I started to worry about her. It was obvious how much she cared for Ice, and I knew she had to be worried sick about him. "You ok, sweetheart?" I asked.

She looked over at me and smiled. "Yeah, I'm ok. Just worrying about what happens next." She paused momentarily and then added, "I'm not sure I can do this, Rebel. Pretending he is dead is going to be a lot harder than I thought. Do you know how all this going to play out?"

She'd asked a very legitimate question, and I'd do my best to answer her. "Well, from what Hawk has told me, he is going to set up a memorial service for the club, all the Chapters, and all Ice's friends. Which will probably be a couple of days from now. Obviously, the whole club will attend. I'm sure he will also invite members from other Chapters to make it look as real as possible. Once the service is over, which will be the hardest part, we will then go about our days without Ice. Keep in mind that Hawk, the girls, you, and I are the only ones that know that he is alive. The rest of the club believes he is dead. So when you are around other members, you are going to have to be on your guard."

"This is not going to be easy," she said, still sounding worried.

"I know, darl'n, but think about how worried you are about him and how much you miss him. That will keep you in the right frame of mind."

"Yeah, I was thinking the same thing. I was trying to think of sad things that would make me cry so that I can shed some tears, too."

"Good girl. You got this! I'm not worried at all."

Just then, Honey walked out into the kitchen, looking like death warmed over. I looked at my watch: 7 am. Pointing at my watch, I said, "See? Like clockwork." Emma and I laughed while Honey looked at us, wondering what in the hell we were laughing at.

"You two are chipper this morning," she said, sounding disgusted. She was definitely not a morning person.

"Yes, we are. You might want to get yourself some coffee and maybe you could join us," I said sarcastically.

"Fuck you, Rebel!"

Shit, that's the second time today that someone said that to me and it's only 7 am! Was it something I said?

Several hours later, Ari emerged looking as beautiful as ever. I thought, *one of these days, real soon, I am going to let her know how I feel about her—but not until the time is right.*

We had a late breakfast and then the girls got ready for their day. I was sitting in the family room when my phone rang. I looked down at the caller ID. It was Hawk.

"Yup," I answered as I stepped outside so that I could talk freely.

"Hey Reb, how are the girls doing?"

"They're good. Getting ready to start their day. What's up?"

"I've made contact with the presidents of all the Chapters and explained to them what's going on. They are all on board. I also told them that we are having a service, biker-style, for Ice next Friday. That's a week away, which gives the Chapters time to travel. I've made all the arrangements and will need to have the girls be ready."

"Got it. Anything else?"

"Yeah. The boys cleaned up the mess at Grayson's house. They torched the house, too, so that will explain why we don't have a body. The Satans will know soon that Grayson is dead. You need to let Ice know."

"You think we will get any blowback from the house being torched?" I asked. Torching the place seemed a little drastic to me, but it definitely would give us a reason to not have a body.

"I've already taken care of that. I've spoken to Briggs. He's going to take care of everything for us."

Jack Briggs was our guy on the force. He knew how to make it work with us, and we respected him for it. He wasn't in our pocket, but he was always willing to help if we needed it, as long as we weren't breaking the law. Well, I guess burning down someone's house was breaking the law, but I was sure that Hawk had told him everything about what that animal had done to Emma. Briggs believed in the law, but he also believed that there were always exceptions to it.

"Good. What do you want the girls to do until the service? Want me to keep them here?" I asked. *Shit, I hope he says no, but I am sure he is gonna say yes. Fuck. I'm going to go stir-crazy.*

"Yeah, I do. They need to lay low until the service. Remember, they are grieving. Our new clubhouse won't be ready for several weeks and Betty's will not be able to accommodate all the people and the food they will be bringing once Ice's death is confirmed. We need a temporary clubhouse in the interim. I don't want folks bringing stuff to Ice's house—I don't want to draw attention there. Got any ideas?"

"What about Kandi's?" It seemed so obvious, I didn't know why we hadn't thought of it sooner. Kandi's was our club, so we wouldn't even need to ask anyone.

"Fuck, that's a great idea. It's a little farther out than I had wanted, but still a good location. Good job, Reb, I should have thought about that myself."

"Hey man, you have had enough to think about. You gonna call Callie?" I asked.

"Yeah, I will give her a heads-up and tell her we're taking over the club for a while. We can keep the strippers working and use the back two convention rooms, along with the private rooms. We'll lose a lot of income from the private rooms, but we'll save in the long run paying rent somewhere."

"You got that right. If you need anything, you know where to find me. You know, me, the Knights of Silence Club Sergeant at Arms and babysitter."

He laughed into the phone. "Don't knock it, brother. At least you can enjoy the scenery," he said.

"Yeah, Hawk, that's the problem. I can look but I can't touch!"

I could hear Hawk laughing as he hung up the phone. *Fucker!*

After I'd finished talking to Hawk, I walked back in the house. The girls were sitting in the great room, chatting. *Shit, don't they ever run out of things to say? What's wrong with just enjoying the silence? I swear I will never figure women out.*

I said, "Hey, girls. I just got off the phone with Hawk. Ice's memorial will be held next Friday."

Honey said, "Rebel, that's over a week away. Why are we waiting so long?"

"We got a lot of members coming from all over; they need travel time," I said. "Hawk has decided to give them that time, and since he's the new prez in the eyes of the outside world, we do what he tells us to do."

Honey just smirked and rolled her eyes.

I continued, "So, as I was saying, the memorial will be held next Friday. We are securing a location at Kandi's to accommodate the members from out of town that will be coming in, as well as using it for a clubhouse until the new one is fitted to meet our needs." I looked over to Honey. "Honey, you will be in charge of coordinating logistics for our guests. Emma, you and Ari can help with that. Honey has a lot of experience handling this, you both can learn a lot from her." The girls nodded and looked at me as if there was more. "What?" I asked.

"Well, what do we do between now and next Friday?" Emma asked.

Was I just speaking another language? Did they not hear a word I just said? "Like I said, you and Ari will be helping Honey with logistics." Emma still looked at me with confusion. I looked over to Honey, pleading with my eyes for some help.

"Emma, dear, what Rebel is saying is that there is going to be a lot of out-of-towners coming in over the next few days. We will work together to ensure that everyone has a place to sleep, that they are fed, and that everyone is comfortable."

"Oh," Emma said, as if she understood.

Isn't that what I just said? I just shook my head. I didn't know what to do with that.

Then Emma added, "Is everyone staying here?"

"No," Honey said. "They will be staying at Kandi's. Which means that we will need to gather up blankets and pillows and get some food. It's gonna be a week, and we better get started."

"Isn't Kandi's that strip club?" Emma asked.

Oh fuck, I don't like where this is going. I like Emma, I really do, but she sure has a lot to learn about being an old lady. Thank God for Honey.

"It is, but there are rooms in the back that we can use. I'm surprised Hawk didn't think of it before, it's perfect as an interim clubhouse," Honey replied.

"Ok, just let me know what you need me to do," Emma said.

"Well, first, why don't you and I sit down and figure out food? Then we can send Ari with Rebel to do some grocery shopping and get it all delivered to Kandi's. Then, you and I can get on the phone with the other old ladies to secure the other items we need. Sound good?"

"Sounds good," Emma replied.

"Yep, sounds good to me," Ari chimed in.

I thought, *I knew Honey could handle all of this. She's gonna make a great old lady someday.*

The girls sat down at the bar and worked on planning food, and I took advantage of the quiet time, grabbing a beer from the fridge and going to sit outside. I needed some time to myself before all the chaos of the next few days arose. Usually I'd be removed from this type of shit, but as babysitter to the girls, I was stuck right dab in the middle of it this time.

One thing I needed to do was get a cage. I really couldn't buy groceries and haul them home on my Harley, with Ari on the back. *Ari on the back of my bike. What a nice thought. I think I will ponder that for a while.* I took a drink of my beer, laid my head back, and just relaxed for whatever time I had at the moment. I'd call Tiny later, after my nap.

CHAPTER 13

Emma

I spent most of the day helping Honey get things arranged and ready for all the bikers coming into town. Tiny had brought over the black pickup truck that he'd used to take me to my apartment so that Rebel and Ari could go get food. A memory of that truck flashed through my head. *That was the day that Mark followed us.* I hadn't known it was Mark at the time, but had found out after we got back to the clubhouse. Suddenly, I became scared and nervous thinking about Mark and had to remind myself that he was dead. Cade had killed him. Brutally.

Will I be able to get past the fact that Caden killed him? It doesn't bother me so much that Caden killed him, anyone could see it was done in self-defense ... well, to an extent. But the way that Caden killed him. I can't get the image of Mark's body hanging in the basement. Am I ever going to get over this? Will I ever feel safe when I see something that reminds me of Mark? I shook my head as if to free myself from the thoughts that plagued my head. I couldn't think about that now. I needed to keep busy.

"Honey, what else do you need me to do?" I asked.

Honey looked at me quizzically. What was wrong? She was giving me the oddest look.

"You're back with us," she said.

"What do you mean? I've been sitting here the entire time," I responded, totally confused by her remark.

"Sweetheart, your body may have been here, but your head was a million miles away." Well, she was right about that. I didn't realize it was so obvious that I had been lost in thought.

"Oh, that. I just have a lot on my mind. Things that I need to deal with."

She walked over to me and gave me a hug. "If you need to talk, I'm here, sweetie. You've been through a lot the last couple of weeks. Nobody can blame you if you are still dealing with the ramifications of all that."

"Thanks, Honey. I really appreciate it and in time, I may just take you up on it." I paused for a moment and then added, "Can I tell you something?"

"Sure, hun."

"I was so jealous of you when I first got back in touch with Caden. I knew I came between you two. I felt bad to an extent, but was more jealous than anything else. You know the man that he is today, and all I had was the boy I had known 20 years ago." I waited for her to say something, but she didn't. Feeling the need to add something, I continued, "And, well, now that I have gotten to know you, I really like you. You've become a good friend to me."

She smiled and said, "Well, that makes us even. I was jealous of you, too. I knew that you and Ice had a history and I guessed that you were the reason he never settled down with anyone. He was never going to make me his old lady. I never realized that until you came."

"I'm sorry." I didn't know what else to say. "I really never meant to hurt anyone by coming back into his life."

"I know that, really I do. I was hurt at first, but I know that you are the one that has been meant for him all along. I've never seen him content, truly content like he is with you. I loved him—hell, I think I still do in a way. But it really makes me happy to see him happy. That's what's important," she said.

"And what about you?"

"Oh, now don't you go worrying about me. I know there's someone out there for me. There has to be, right?" she asked with a laugh.

"I know there is!" I said confidently. "What will you do now? Will you stay with the club?"

"Ice has assured me that I will always have a place with the club. He has told me over and over again that this club is my home. So, I plan on sticking around. Besides, I really enjoy taking care of these boys and I do consider you a friend." She let the silence between us settle and then said, "You know, he took me in when I had nothing. I will never forget what Ice and this club have done for me."

"What happened to you before you came to the club?" I asked. I had always wondered how she'd gotten involved with the club.

"That, my dear Emma, is a story for another day. Right now, we have work to do." She was right. I decided not to push the issue. I figured she would tell me when she was ready.

"Can I ask another question?" I added.

"Sure hun," she replied.

"Is Honey your real name?" She laughed, and in a way it did seem a bit odd to ask, but I was curious and I wanted to know.

"No, It's Amanda. The boys gave me the name "Honey" and it kinda stuck." She paused for a moment and then looked at me oddly and said, "Did I really just say that?" And we both started laughing.

Just then, Hawk walked through the front door. "Hey, girls. How are things going here?" he asked. He looked at me and then over to Honey. *Oh my God, did he just blush? Is Hawk crushing on Honey? I wonder if she knows.* This was definitely something to get my mind off of everything. When I was hiding out with Rebel I had made a pact to myself that I was going to find him a nice girl. But after seeing him and Ari together, it looked like he had already found her. So I decided that my new mission was to hook up Honey and Hawk. *It has a nice ring to it, doesn't it?* I asked myself. Just then I noticed both of them staring at me curiously. "What?" I asked.

"What's going on in the head of yours, Emma?" Honey asked.

"Not a thing," I replied smugly. "Don't you need to tell Hawk about all the arrangements we've made today?"

And just like that, it was like I was no longer in the room. Honey and Hawk went over all the details and arrangements and I just sat there watching the two of them. I don't know why I didn't see their connection before.

A couple of hours later, not long after Hawk had left, Ari and Rebel returned empty-handed. As if he could read my mind, Rebel said, "We dropped everything off at Kandi's. Thought it was pointless to carry everything in here, only to pack it up again to take it there. Don't ya think?"

"Good thinking," said Honey.

"We did get a few things for here for the next few days. I'll carry those in now," he said as he headed out the door.

"I'll help," said Ari as she rushed out the door to help him.

After she walked out of the door, I turned to Honey and said, "So what's up with those two?" It seemed obvious to me that there was some type of connection between them, but I wasn't sure if I was imagining it or if it was real. If it was real, they'd been doing a good job hiding it.

"Oh, those two have had a thing for each other since Ice brought Rebel into the club." Honey rolled her eyes as if annoyed. "I just wish they would be honest with each other about their feelings and sort their issues out." She added, "Rebel has been dancing around his feelings for her for as long as I can remember. He's worried that Ice will beat the shit out of him if he messes with his sister. I can't say I really blame him, but at least he could ask him. Don't ya think?"

Now it was making sense. *Would Caden really keep them from being together if they truly loved each other? The Caden I knew 20 years ago wouldn't, but the Caden today? I don't know.* I thought about it for a minute and decided that yeah, he most definitely would. "He should ask him. What could it hurt?"

"For most people, it couldn't. But if Ice is totally against the idea, he could get so pissed off that Rebel would even think about dating his kid sister that he'd beat the shit out of him. And Ice would win. That's why Rebel is scared."

"Would he really hurt him, just for that?" I asked curiously.

"Hell yeah, he would. That's almost as bad as one of the guys going after his old lady," she said. My first thought was that that was crazy, but then I realized that Caden was very protective of what's his in a rather barbaric way.

Just then, Rebel and Ari came back in carrying a few bags. I thought about what Honey had said. When the time was right, I was going to encourage Rebel to talk to Caden. It was obvious that Caden respected and trusted Rebel, so why wouldn't he trust him with his sister?

As I started to empty the bags that Rebel placed on the counter, Ari came up behind me, dropped her bags on the counter and went into the bedroom, slamming the door behind her. I looked over to Honey and again, she rolled her eyes. She wasn't kidding. There was a lot of tension between the two of them. I looked over at Rebel, who looked defeated. He didn't say anything, just went outside. Suddenly, I found myself feeling sorry for him and Ari.

CHAPTER 14

Rebel

Fuck! That girl gets pissed off faster than any chick I know. I couldn't stop pacing back and forth, trying to figure out what just happened. I didn't get it. I was about to tell Ari how I felt about her, but before I could say the words, she said, "Fire, don't. I can't hear that right now." And then she turned and walked back in the house. What had I done? What had I said?

I followed her into the house, hoping that she would clue me in to what the problem was, but no. Instead, she plopped the groceries on the counter, stomped off to her room, and slammed the door. *I swear, I can't win. I need a drink. I need a smoke. Fuck it, I need a drink and a smoke. Damn woman.* I hadn't had a smoke in two weeks. I carried a pack with me to remind me not to have one, and just one confrontation with Ari was making me want one. I had no damn willpower.

I walk back in the house and headed straight for the bar. As I rummaged through the bottles, I found Ice's bottle of Maker's Mark. I grabbed a shot glass, poured a shot, and downed it. I poured myself another one, downed it, and proceeded to go back outside to have my smoke.

"Everything ok, Rebel?" Emma asked.

"Oh, it's just peachy!" I replied as I headed out the door.

I pulled out the unopened pack of smokes, knowing that once I opened it there would be no turning back. I wouldn't have the courage to toss them, and I would smoke the other nineteen in the pack. *Fuck it. She drives me nuts.*

I lit the cigarette and took a drag. Already I could feel the tension leaving my body. *Why do cigarettes have to taste so good?* Just then, my phone rang. I pulled it out of my pocket and checked to see who it is. *Fuck! It's Ari. She is in the house, in her room, and she's still calling me on my fucking phone. Why doesn't she just come out here and talk to me? Shit.* "What?" I said after answering the phone.

"I'm sorry," she said into the phone.

"For what, Ari?!" I wasn't about to give her any slack. She'd pissed me off, and I was gonna make damn sure she knew it.

"You were trying to tell me something and I wouldn't let you. I'm sorry," she said.

"It's fine, Ari. At least now I know where I stand. No worries, doll, I'm good." I wasn't going to give her the satisfaction of knowing that it had affected me in any way.

"Will you tell me what you were going to say?" she asked.

"Fuck no! You had your chance, Ari. Why wouldn't you listen to me fifteen minutes ago?"

"I was scared," she whispered into the phone.

"What in the hell are you scared of, Ari?" I asked. I had to know. She'd known me ever since I met her brother at Dirty Dick's that night we took out five Satans—what could she be afraid of? She was quiet for a while and I started getting frustrated with her. Why wouldn't she speak? I said, "Ari, you gotta tell me. If you are scared of something, I need to know."

"I'm afraid that you feel the same way about me as I feel about you," she said.

"And what is wrong with that?" I asked. She was being ridiculous.

"Because I don't think my brother would approve," she said meekly. "I don't want to get my hopes up about us if Caden is going to screw it up."

Now we were getting somewhere. I said, "What if I told you that I have already talked to your brother?"

"You have?" she asked, eagerly. "What did he say?"

"As long as I don't break your heart, I will stay alive. Does that work for you?" I waited for a response, but she didn't say anything. I said, "Now why don't you get your cute little ass out here and talk to me." Still nothing—but a few seconds later, she came walking out the door, phone in hand and tears in her eyes. She just stood on the porch, staring at me.

I held out my arms, inviting her in. "Come here, darl'n," I said. She came running into my arms. Finally, I was able to hold the woman I loved. The feeling was euphoric, and I didn't want the moment to end. "So, I take it that you feel the same way I do?" I asked.

"I don't know. You haven't told me exactly how you feel about me."

Fuck, she is going to make me work for this now. Damn woman. Out loud I said, "I love you, Ari. Hell, I have loved you from the moment your brother introduced you to me three years ago. I know it has only been three years, but I don't remember a time when you weren't a part of my life. Holding you like this is something that I want to do for the rest of my life."

Tears streamed down her face as she clung to my shirt. I just held her and let her cry. Five minutes went by without her saying a word. Had I said the wrong thing? Was it too much, too soon?

She pulled away, wiping the tears from her eyes, and said, "I love you too, Fire! And I always have. I can't tell you how many times I've dreamed about you, about being with you."

I like the sound of that. When this shit is done and we actually get some alone time, I'm definitely taking her up on that offer!

We went back into the house, both of us much happier. Now that all that was settled between us, we could get this other shit done and go on with our lives.

"You two finally kiss and make up?" Honey asked in that damn motherly tone that she had. That woman never missed a trick.

"Yeah," I said. "We're all good here."

Ari looking at me lovingly and said, "Yep, all good."

The rest of the day and night was pretty quiet. We had another amazing dinner provided by our very own master chef, Honey. The girls chatted, played some cards, and then finally, they all headed to bed. The house was quiet. I did one final check around the house and headed to bed myself. It had been a long day.

CHAPTER 15

Emma

The previous week had been a whirlwind of things to do. Honey, Ari and I had worked on preparing food that we could freeze and store at Kandi's. The out-of-town guests began arriving, and Rebel and Hawk were constantly in and out taking care of things on their end. Finally, it was the day of Caden's memorial service. I couldn't help but feel sad. I knew it was dumb, since he was alive and well, but I kept imagining what it would be like if he wasn't, if it was all real. I wouldn't be able to bear losing him, not after all we'd been through—and especially not now that we had found our way back to each other. We had a future. We would have a family. I prayed every day for God to keep him safe.

Dressed all in black, I took a deep breath and made my way downstairs. Rebel was up and ready, dressed in black jeans, a black t-shirt, and his cut. Apparently bikers didn't really dress up for funerals. I looked down at the black dress I was wearing and thought perhaps I was overdressed. Before I could ask, Rebel said, "You look beautiful, Emma. But if I were you, I would not be wearing a dress."

"Oh. I'm too dressed up, aren't I?" I asked.

"No, you look great. But you will be riding on the back of Hawk's bike today in the procession. Probably not a good idea to wear a dress."

"Why? Why am I going to be on a bike?" I asked nervously. I'd only been on a motorcycle one time, the night Rebel brought me here. And I was terrified! Cade had said he would take me out on his bike, but with all the stuff that had been going on, it had never happened.

"Because, Emma, you are Ice's old lady. You ride in the procession. Since Hawk is the new President, you ride with him. Ari rides with me next in line, since I'm the Sergeant at Arms."

"Rebel, I've never been on a bike before. I didn't know this. I can't. I just can't do it," I said nervously.

"It's tradition, Emma. And one thing I have learned over the years is that you don't mess with biker traditions." He waited for me to say something, but I just stood there looking panicked. "Don't worry, darl'n, it'll be fine. But I suggest you put on something more appropriate."

I nodded, still very unsure. I thought, *maybe I can call Hawk and see if we could drive in a car instead of his bike.* Then I remembered that this was all for Caden. *I can do this.* I turned and marched myself back upstairs to change. *I can do this,* I repeated to myself several times. *I can do this.*

I changed into a pair of black jeans, boots, and a black sweater. I braided my hair down the back instead of wearing it down and grabbed my leather jacket. I looked at myself in the mirror and realized: I was a biker chick! I'd never thought I would be living in the biker world, but there I was. And although there was danger, I had Caden. It was all worth it, and I wouldn't have had it any other way.

I went back downstairs and Rebel nodded, giving me his approval. By then Honey and Ari were dressed and ready to go as well. We were all wearing black and ready to play our parts.

"So Rebel, how is this gonna work?" I asked.

"Well, Tiny will be here to drive the truck. You and Honey will ride over to the church with him. Ari will ride with me. There will be a service at the church—a short one, hopefully—but brothers will be invited to speak and say something about Ice. That alone could prolong the service. Once the service is completed, the procession will begin. All the brothers—and when I say all the brothers, I don't mean just this club—will line up. Spike, our road captain, will lead, followed by Hawk and me. All the brothers from our Chapter will fall in line next, then all the others."

I knew from that last couple of days that at least 100 bikers had arrived from out of town. We didn't have enough room for everyone at Kandi's and had needed to arrange a block of rooms at the Comfort Suites. That had been a chore in itself. It felt like we'd taken over the whole hotel.

"Thanks, Rebel."

"You ready for this?" he asked, looking at all three of us.

"I'm ready," I replied. Honey and Ari nodded in agreement.

Just then we heard a bike pull up. A few minutes later, Tiny came in. It was time to go. I looked over to Honey and Ari. They actually looked sad enough to be going to a funeral. Looking at their faces, I realized that I was ready, too. Just the thought that this could be real made me sad.

We all headed out the door and proceeded to the Broken Chains Church, a nondenominational biker church. I didn't know much about it, but from what I had gathered from Hawk, it was where the club held all its weddings and memorial services.

We entered the church and it was completely full. I was in awe at the number of people who were there to pay their respects to Caden. It was overwhelming. Hawk was waiting for us at the door and proceeded to walk us up to the front pew. He sat with us as we waited for the service to begin. As I sat there, I looked around the altar and finally caught a glimpse of the all-black casket situated directly in front. I had not even noticed it before, but seeing it there now, I couldn't hold back my tears. I knew Caden wasn't in there, but the thought that he could be one day brought me to tears. The casket was closed, which I had expected. They just needed something for show.

The service began like any other memorial service that I had attended. The pastor said a few prayers and the body was blessed.

Then the pastor invited people to get up and speak. Hawk rose and walked up to the pulpit.

"Ice was not only my president and brother, he was my best friend," Hawk started. "We have been to hell and back together, we rose through the ranks in the club together ... and now, it is time to say goodbye. I make a pledge to you, my brother and my friend: I will protect this club, your old lady, and your sister. I'll keep this family whole. Four wheels move the body, two wheels move the soul." He paused for a moment, wiped his eyes and then continued with a poem.

As you ride the lonely road,
Feeling the wind in heaven,
Can you hear us down on Earth,
Weeping for you as you go,
Wishing we could take you home?
As you ride the lonely road
We'll lay your body down.
Can you hear me call your name?
Can you see our falling tears?
They say Heaven has no tears,
So maybe you can't see us here.
As you ride the lonely road
I'll ride along the earthen road
Filled with memories of you
And all the roads you rode with me.
Can you hear the sound of silence
Where once your bike rolled with
mine? As you ride the lonely road
Life will take me here and there.
Can you feel the pain inside
As I see you here no more?
The silence where you once spoke
Screams so loud it's hard to bear.
Your leather and your bike
Now they gather dust
And we carry the empty space

That's the shape of you.
As you ride the lonely road,
Watch for me as you go.
One day I'll be there.
I will shake your hand
And ride with you along the only road that has no end.[iii]

He paused, then added, "RIP, brother." Everyone in the church repeated him. At that moment I realized that everyone there was not just a member of Caden's club—they were also members of Caden's family. Every one of those people respected and loved him.

Hawk stepped down and returned to his seat next to me. Several other brothers spoke, and every one of them ended with, "RIP, brother." And every time it was said, the entire church repeated their words.

Suddenly, the door at the back of the church opened. Everyone turned to see who it was, watching as four Satans entered the church and sat down in one of the pews in the back row. I glanced over at Hawk, and for the first time, I saw actual worry on his face. I leaned over and whispered in his ear, "Is everything ok?" He nodded unconvincingly. We turned back to the front of the church and continued to listen to the remainder of the service.

When everything was said and done, six members of Cade's club walked up to the casket, lifted it, and proceeded to carry it out of the church. I recognized some of them: Spike, Dbag, and Tiny. Hawk, Honey, Rebel, Ari and I were the first to leave the church, following directly behind the casket. Everyone else followed behind us. When we passed the Satans seated in the back, the one with the word *President* on his cut nodded at me. I barely nodded back and proceeded to walk, looking down.

When we got outside, I was amazed to see dozens of bikes parked in formation starting at the entrance of the parking lot. *Who did this?* I thought to myself. There were over one hundred bikes in the parking lot, all in formation and ready to head out. Leading the way was a police car and the hearse. Behind them was a lone bike, which I assumed was the road captain's bike. All the others were lined behind. It was quite a sight to see.

"Emma, you wait here with Rebel and Ari. I'll be right back," Hawk said to me. He turned and went back inside. I guessed that he was going to talk to the surprise guests.

A few minutes later, he returned. "Everything ok?" I asked.

"Yep. Had a chat with our late arrivals. Just wanted to make sure they weren't planning any trouble. They said that they just wanted to pay their respects."

I looked at him curiously, as if to say, *Really?*

He added, "I took them at their word, Emma. They are far outnumbered here, so if they cause any trouble, they'll be the ones who end up in trouble. I thanked them and came back out here."

He was right. I may not have been an expert at this sort of thing, but it was clear that the Satans were outnumbered. They would be fools to start something at the church. Maybe they just had to see for themselves that Ice was really dead. For all intents and purposes, it was looking like Caden's plan had worked. I thought, *maybe this means he will come home sooner.*

Once the casket was carefully placed in the hearse, we proceeded to the bikes. Spike walked to the lead bike. As we approached the bikes, I started to get nervous. Rebel could see my concern and leaned over to say, "It's gonna be ok, Emma. Hawk's got this." I nodded and followed Hawk to his bike.

Standing next to his bike was a police officer. As we approached, Hawk shook the officer's hand. "Sgt. Briggs, this is Emma Baylee, Ice's old lady," Hawk said.

Sgt. Briggs offered his hand and said, "I'm very sorry for your loss."

"Thank you," I replied demurely.

Sgt. Briggs turned toward Hawk and asked, "Helmets?"

Hawk shook his head. "No." I looked at Hawk curiously. He answered my unspoken question, saying, "Riding without helmets during the procession, Emma, is a sign of respect to Ice."

"But isn't it illegal? Aren't there helmet laws?" I asked.

"Yes, but the law is usually overlooked during funeral processions. Wearing a helmet is like wearing a hat. Same concept," he replied.

Standing beside his bike, Spike started his engine. Hawk, Rebel, and all the other bikers in the procession did the same while standing beside their bikes. Then Spike revved his engine five times, followed again by everyone else. The sound was powerful and soulful all at the same time. Once everyone had stopped, I heard one last rev. When everything was silent, everyone mounted their bikes. The hearse departed, and all the bikes followed in unison. When I looked behind me the site before my eyes was unlike anything I had ever seen. Motorcycles followed and I was unable to see where they ended. They just kept coming as we drove slowly through town. The outpouring of support for Caden was overwhelming and brought tears to my eyes. It was obvious that all these people respected and loved him. When we arrived at Kandi's the hearse turned around and headed back toward town.

Caden

It was surreal watching my own funeral service. I have to admit, I was surprised by the turnout. For a minute, I let my ego get the best of me and was fucking proud that so many people were there. For a minute. Then reality sank in when I saw the Satans arrive. What the fuck were they doing there? I hoped they were just there to obtain proof that I was already dead. Their showing up reminded me that I needed to forge a plan on how I was going to approach them.

CHAPTER 16

Emma

After every funeral service I'd attended in the past, close friends of the family would all meet at a designated location for a meal—in most cases, at the family of the deceased's house. Friends and family would talk fondly about the person that passed, but it was always a solemn affair. The gathering at Kandi's was a full-blown party, nothing like what I had been used to. There were so many people there drinking and partying that at times it made me angry. *How could they be so happy?* I thought to myself. I knew that Caden was still alive, but they didn't.

As I walked through the crowd of people, I overheard some people talking about him. They were telling stories and remembering him. I realized then that they were not celebrating his death, they were celebrating his life. After that realization, I began to relax and join in on the celebration.

The party progressed into the night and it began getting late. By then I was ready to go back to Caden's house. Hawk approached me and said, "You doing ok, sweetheart?"

I smiled and said, "Yeah, I'm just a little tired."

"I bet you are. How about I have one of the prospects take you home? This party is sure to go into the late hours of the night, and you are most definitely not expected to stay for the duration."

I thought about it for a minute and then nodded. "I'd like that. What about Ari and Honey? Are they going to stay?"

He looked around the room and said, "Let me see if they are ready to go. Hang tight for a minute." He stepped away.

A few minutes later he came back with Rebel, Tiny, and Ari. "Honey is going to stick around for a while. I'll make sure she gets home safe. Tiny is going to take you back in the truck, and Rebel and Ari are going to go on his bike. I want Rebel to stay with you both, so he will remain at the house."

I looked over to Rebel and said, "I'm sorry for ruining your night, Rebel."

He glanced at Ari and replied, "I'm not. I'm ready to go too."

"Alright then," I said. I glanced at Tiny and continued, "I'm ready when you are."

"Then let's go, Miss Emma," he replied.

Why does he insist on calling me Miss Emma? I've told him so many times to just call me Emma, but he never does. I give up.

About thirty minutes later we were pulling into the driveway at Caden's house. I realized I needed to stop thinking about the house as just Caden's house—after what Hawk told me and my conversation with Cade the other night, it was clear that it was now my house, too.

As we walked into the house, my cell phone started to ring. The day before, Rebel had taken me to the Verizon store to get a new phone. Luckily, all of my contacts and pictures were backed up, so I was able to get everything back. I looked at the caller id: my mom was calling. *Holy shit, I haven't spoken to her in two weeks! I need to answer this.*

"Hey, Mom. How are you?" I said into the phone.

"Emma, where have you been? I've been trying to reach you for two weeks. Your father and I have been so worried," she said.

"I know, Mom, I'm sorry. Things have been really crazy for me and I'm really sorry for not calling you to check in."

"Sweetheart, you never returned my calls or my texts. That's not like you."

"I lost my phone, and I just got a new one yesterday. But I should have called. My bad."

"So everything is alright?" she asked. She added, "You said things have been crazy. What's going on?"

"Mom, I can't go into the details right now. Just know that I am ok. No, actually, I'm not ok, I'm great! I have so much to tell you and Dad, but I can't right now. I promise, when the dust settles and things get back to normal, I will fill you both in on everything."

I could tell that she wanted to press me for information, but she didn't. She was quiet for a moment and then said, "Ok, dear. As long as you are ok." She paused and then added, "Why don't you come by Sunday for dinner? We'd love to see you."

"That's not going to work, Mom, but I promise I'll come by soon. I have to go now. I love you. Please give Dad my love too."

Sounding a bit annoyed, she replied hesitantly, "Okay, dear. Take care of yourself and don't be a stranger. We love you too."

I'd done my best to appease my mom, but I also wanted to rush her off the phone. Still, she was right; I should have at least let her know I was ok. I'd just gotten so wrapped up in everything going on that the thought had never crossed my mind.

After I hung up the phone, I noticed Rebel looking at me curiously. "What?" I asked.

He smiled. "Nothing. I was just thinking how nice it would be to talk to my mom," he replied.

"Well, why don't you call her?" I asked. Just then, Ari reached over to him and touched his arm. He glanced at her warmly, then put his hand over hers and held it there. It was such a sweet gesture that it almost brought tears to my eyes.

"I can't," he said sadly.

I thought, *Oh no, I didn't even think when I said that. Has his mom passed away?*

He then added, "I haven't spoken to either of my parents in almost four years now. Not because of anything that went down between us, just because of things back home that they are involved in." He paused, then continued, "I don't even know if they are still alive."

"Oh Rebel, I'm so sorry. I didn't know."

"It's ok. When my parents sent me to the US, they thought it was for the best. They are heavily involved in the Irish Republican Army, and they just didn't think it would be the best environment for a young man. I guess they wanted better for me or something.

They contacted Ace, and with his help, I came here. Unfortunately, by the time I actually got to the states, Ace had already been killed. That's when I met Ice," he said.

"Hawk told me about the night you and Caden met." I left it at that, I really didn't want to bring up the details of that night. He didn't say anything about it either. "So why haven't you called your mom or dad?" I asked.

"I've tried, but the numbers I had for them are no longer working. Shit was going down big time when I left and I am sure they had to change all their contact information as a result. I worry about them, but I am sure that someday I will see them again, either here or in Belfast."

"I hope so too." I hadn't known any of this about Rebel. It went a long way towards explaining why he always seemed so different from the other brothers in the club.

"Well, if you two don't mind, I think I am going to go to bed. I'm beat," I said to Rebel and Ari. "Sweet dreams, you two."

I was already halfway up the stairs when they replied, "Sweet dreams, Emma."

CHAPTER 17

Rebel

After Emma went to bed, I got up from the barstool that I was sitting on and stood next to Ari. Holding out my hand, I said, "Hey beautiful, why don't you come sit with me on the couch for a bit?" Without hesitation, she took my hand and we walked over to the couch. I situated myself in the corner and she snuggled up against me. We sat there for several minutes, finally able to relax after all the chaos of the last few days. I was enjoying the quiet, enjoying having my girl lying here with me. I'd never had that before.

"I'm sorry about your mom and dad," Ari whispered.

I pulled her closer into a hug and said, "Don't be, sweetheart. They are very passionate about what they're doing. It's the life they have chosen. I don't begrudge them anything and I know that they are still alive. I will see them again."

"I know, but it just makes me sad that you are alone."

"Baby, I am far from alone. I have you, first and foremost, but I also have the club. That's a pretty big fucking family if you ask me. Don't ya think?" I asked.

"Yeah, I guess you are right." She paused for a moment and then added, "It kinda reminds me of Caden and me when our parents died. We didn't have anybody either, and then the club came along and we had this huge family. I didn't understand it all back then; I was only ten. But now, after all these years, I realize that this entire club, all these brothers and old ladies, they really are my family."

"You got that right, darl'n. And there is not one person who belongs to this club that would not lay down their life for you or your brother."

"I know." She snuggled up closer to me and all I could think about was taking her to bed. However, the timing was way off. It was not where I wanted our first time to be. I wanted it to be special for us both. Not in her brother's house, where we'd be sharing it with the rest of the world. So it wasn't happening. Instead, I leaned down and kissed her on her head.

We sat there for several minutes and then her breathing changed. She had fallen asleep. I eased my way out from beneath her and she woke, but barely. It was like she was still asleep, only with her eyes open. I scooped her up into my arms and carried her off to bed.

I laid her down on the bed and she stirred slightly. I turned to leave and heard her murmur in her sleep, "Please don't go, Fire." Everything inside of me wanted to stay, but I felt that it was important for Ice to hear about my relationship with Ari from me first. Any other way just didn't seem right.

I walked over to the bed and kissed her on the cheek. "Not tonight, beautiful. Sweet dreams." I watched her for a couple of minutes, thinking, *what a lucky son of a bitch I am that this beautiful woman loves me. I will make damn sure that I am worthy of her every day for the rest of my life.*

I stepped out of Ari's room just as Hawk and Honey were walking in the front door. Hawk looked at me curiously, as if I was up to no good. It pissed me off. He had no right jumping to conclusions. Defensively, I asked, "What?!"

"Isn't that Ari's room you just walked out of?" he asked smugly.

"Fuck you, Hawk. She fell asleep on the couch. I carried her to bed. End of story. Get your fuckin' mind out of the gutter."

"Yeah, right. Wait until Ice finds out you have been banging his sister."

Hawk was really pissing me off. At that moment, I didn't care if he was my acting president or my vice president, he was talking about shit he didn't know anything about. I got up in his face and said, "Look, motherfucker. You're talking about stuff you know nothing about. Until you get your facts straight, I suggest you keep your fuckin' mouth shut. You got me?"

Hawk pushed me away and said angrily, "You better remember who you are talking to."

"Fuck you! I don't give a fuck who you are, and neither will Ice—especially if he hears you talking shit about his kid sister."

He started to speak, but Honey jumped between us and said, "Boys, enough! Hawk, get yourself a beer and cool off. Rebel, you pour yourself a drink, too. You are both acting like a couple of ten-year-olds. Enough is enough! Ice would be pissed at you both, hearing you talk like this." She looked over at me and said, "Grow up, Rebel!" She then turned to Hawk and said, "And you! Go get laid and unwind. You have been wound tighter than a fucking top recently." She scowled at both of us and added, "If you two don't straighten up, I'll put you both over my knee. And don't think I can't do it!" She stomped off towards her bedroom.

Hawk got himself a beer and sat down at the bar. He said, "Hey man, she's right. I'm sorry, brother. I jumped to conclusions and I shouldn't have. And I do fucking need to get laid!"

"Fuck, we both do!" I agreed.

"We cool?" he asked.

"Yeah, bro, we're cool." I sat down at the bar with a shot of bourbon. "So, how was the rest of the party?"

Shaking his head, he said, "Still fucking going on. Those fuckers like to party. But Honey was ready to go, and I was getting tired myself. I can't party like that anymore, I'm too fucking old." He laughed.

"You got that right, old man!" I said.

"Fuck you, Rebel!" he said.

"Hey, remember what Honey said—you don't want her coming out here and putting you over her knee!" I laughed.

He shrugged. Under his breath, he muttered, "Maybe I do."

Well hell, I didn't see that coming. I figured it would probably be best if I did not respond to that. Hopefully he'd be able to work that shit out.

We finished our drinks in silence, and then Hawk got up to leave. "Catch ya later, bro."

"Yeah man, see you tomorrow."

After Hawk left, I did my final check on the house. When I was sure the girls were locked in safely, I turned in myself. It had been a long and exhausting day.

CHAPTER 18

Caden

It'd been several weeks since my memorial service, and the time away from my family was killing me. But I knew how important it was to lay low during this time. I had spoken to Rebel several times, just to check in and see how the girls were doing. He'd assured me that they were in good hands. I'd also been watching the Satans, learning their routines and looking for the most opportune time to make contact with Gypsy, their president.

After watching them for several days, I decided my best bet would be to have Hawk set up a meet with them. As much as I wanted it to be just Gypsy and me, I knew others would have to be there too. If I just approached him and caught him off guard, I could easily find myself dead before I even had a chance to talk to him.

Before I let Hawk and Rebel in on my plan, I had to think through every detail. Nothing could go wrong with this. Too much was riding on it, including my life and my future. I went back to the shithole hotel I was staying at and began working things out. When I was finally comfortable with the majority of my plan, I called Rebel. He answered on the first ring.

"The girls are fine!" he said, exasperated.

Fuck him, I don't check in that much. Do I? Hell, I probably do. It must drive him absolutely insane. Well, fuck that shit. Those three girls mean the world to me.

"Fuck you! That's not why I'm calling, asshole," I said into the phone. "I'm ready to make my move with the Satans, but I need your and Hawk's help. Meet me at the Motel 6 in Wattsburg at noon. I'm in room 24. Park your bikes in the back and try not to draw any attention to yourselves. Or better yet, come in the truck."

"I think you are being a little paranoid, man," Rebel said.

Sure, that's easy for him to say. It's not his life on the line.

"Never mind how paranoid I'm being. You can never be too careful. I'll see you both at noon." I hung up the phone.

I had a few hours to get some sleep. I'd been up all night playing this out in my head and on the shitty notepaper the hotel provided. It had to work. It just had to.

Three hours later, my alarm went off. It was time to get up and get this shit done. I showered and got ready, waiting for my boys. At 12:05, there was a knock on the door. I looked out, it was them. I opened the door, and before I could catch my breath, Hawk pulled me into an embrace. "What the hell, man?" I said.

He backed away, cleared his throat, and said, "Hey, sorry. It's just good to see you alive and well. I mean, I knew you were alive, but going through all the motions the last several weeks, planning your wake ... well, it just fucks with your head. Ya know?" Rebel and I stared at Hawk, and then we both started to laugh.

"You're such a pussy!" I said as I continued to laugh.

"Fuck you both!" Hawk said. "I don't give a shit what you guys think. So I'm a fucking pussy for being glad that my best friend and prez is alive. I'll admit it."

Damn, he needs to get laid, I thought to myself. He was wound tighter than a fucking top.

"Take a seat." I gestured to the luxury seating I had in my posh hotel room: two kitchen-type metal chairs around a very small table with nicks and chips on the table in various locations, a very uncomfortable living room chair, and a single bed with an obvious hole in the center. "I've been thinking about this for the last several days now, and I think it would be best if Hawk makes contact with Gypsy. Call him and set up a meet. Tell him that you want to discuss the future of our two clubs. Try to be diplomatic, but encourage him not to bring his entire entourage. I don't want a fucking army there. But make sure Skid is there." I looked over to Rebel. "I want you at this meeting, brother." I thought for a moment and then added, "Ryder too. Nobody else."

"And what am I supposed to discuss at this meeting?" Hawk asked.

"Yeah, Ice, what's this meeting gonna be about?" Rebel asked.

"You are not going to discuss anything. I am. You are just gonna get them there. The last thing I need to do is take Gypsy off guard. He thinks I'm dead. I can't just walk up to him on the fucking street."

"So you are going to be at this meeting as well?" Hawk asked.

"Oh yeah, I'll be there. We need to pick neutral territory. Any suggestions?" I asked.

"What about Kandi's?" Rebel suggested.

I shook my head. "Not very neutral territory for the Satans."

"Oh yeah, right," Rebel said.

"What about Jimmy's? Don't they have an old warehouse behind them that is abandoned? I think Jimmy owns it. We can secure the warehouse, and it would definitely give us privacy. And Jimmy's is in neutral territory."

I nodded. "That could work. It's neutral, and I think both clubs would feel safe there. Set it up!"

They both looked at me like I had lost my fucking mind. "What?" I asked.

"This meeting is all well and good, but what the fuck are we meeting about? And whatever it is, don't you think we need to take it to the table and discuss it with the club?" Hawk asked.

They had a point. My mind had been so consumed with getting all this straightened out, I'd totally forgotten that I had others to consider. "You're right, man. Fuck. I've been so focused on getting back to the land of the living that I forgot about everything else." I paused for a moment then continued. "I want this meeting to serve two purposes. First of all, I want the Satans to know that I killed Grayson and why. I've been watching them closely over the last several weeks, and they don't seem to be too shook up about his death. I believe that Grayson was a thorn in their side. If I am guessing right, they are glad to be rid of him. The only exception to that might be Gypsy and Skid. But I think we can get through to them. Secondly, I want to end this feud between the clubs."

"And how do you expect to do that? We've been trying to keep the peace for years and nothing has worked," Rebel said.

"We have, but we've missed something. All along, what is the one thing that the Satans have always wanted?" I asked them.

They both looked at each other and Hawk spoke first, "Territory?"

"Wrong," I said. "If my thinking is right, they gave up on trying to obtain our territory years ago. It's too broad, and we are too big for them to overcome."

Rebel said, "Then what do they fucking want?"

"Money," I replied.

"So they want a piece of the guns and drugs?" Hawk asked.

"You got it. It's gonna be your job to sell this to the rest of the club. Convince them that we don't need all the income from these alliances. How good it would be to get out of the dirty shit. We have plenty of legitimate establishments to finance this club, and we can always grow more. We have the people and the resources." I let what I was saying sink in and then continued, "I want us out of guns. I've wanted it for a long time. I want our brothers and their families to stop worrying about the safety of their families. I want to keep us whole and out of jail."

They were both quiet for a couple of minutes and I just let the silence sit between us.

"The club is not going to be happy about the loss of income," Rebel said, shaking his head. "Hell, I don't know if I can handle the cut myself."

"I know. That is why I am planning on making us a silent partner. Let the Satans run the guns and drugs. Let them do the dirty work. We'll get a piece of the action for giving them the business. It keeps the ATF off our backs and keeps our hands a little cleaner. It's a win-win for all of us."

"You think they will go for it?" Rebel asked.

"I do. I think the cut in pay will be hard to swallow at first, but the benefits in the long run will win out. I'm counting on you both to sell it to them. Then once they all agree, we are free to set up the meeting with the Satans," I replied. "You guys good with this?" I asked.

They both looked at each other. Rebel agreed with a nod. "I'm good too," said Hawk. "It will be good to explore more legitimate opportunities. Speaking of which, I've got an idea to run by you when you get back."

"What? Who knows when this shit will end? If it is something that gets us on the right track, tell me now. At this point, nothing can hurt."

"What about porn or escorts? I mean, it's not clean, but it is legal. And the money can be really good," Hawk said.

"You might have something there. I'm game. Run it by the club. If they are on board, start the legwork on it," I said. Hawk nodded. It was a good idea; I was surprised I hadn't thought of it myself. "Are we done here?" I asked.

"Unless you have something else you need, I think we are good," Hawk said. "Rebel?"

"Yep, I'm good," he replied.

"Ok boys, I'm counting on you both. This is a big step for the club. Let's make it happen."

They both nodded in agreement and got up to leave. "Call me if you need anything," Rebel added.

"You know I will. Thanks!"

After they left, I had nothing left to do but to sit and wait—one thing that I was definitely not good at. But sometimes it was all I could do. I was worried about how the club would react to my proposal, but I trusted Hawk and Rebel to help them understand that this was the best move for the club. I hoped they would see it too.

CHAPTER 19

Rebel

On the way back to Edinboro, Hawk called the boys and told them that we were having church at Kandi's in two hours. He wasn't wasting any time getting things done. I was convinced he didn't like being President and was anxious for Ice to come back. I felt the same way. Ice provided the club with good, solid leadership ... and although Hawk was a good guy, Ice just had a way about him that got shit done.

We got to Kandi's about forty-five minutes after we left Ice. We both grabbed some food and drinks, and then waited for the rest of the club to arrive. Some of the boys were already there, enjoying the afternoon show. Some of those guys never did anything but watch naked women dance on a stage. Not that that was a bad thing ... but I had a life, and sex didn't consume me. Not to mention the fact that I had my own beautiful babe. I didn't need any substitutes when I had the best damn girl on the planet.

When all the boys arrived, we all went back to the back meeting room. I was really curious about how this was going to go. These guys relied on the income that we received from the illegal shit, so I would be surprised if they were willing to take a pay cut. However, I hadn't wanted to tell Ice that. Nobody likes negativity, but especially Ice. He was counting on Hawk and me to do this, and I didn't want to let him down.

After everyone was seated, Hawk opened up the meeting. "The memorial service was a tough day for all of us, saying goodbye to Ice and the last few weeks without him, but business doesn't stop for us to mourn. I've got something I want to run by you all, and I want you all to keep an open mind until I'm done. Ok?" They all nodded in agreement and Hawk continued. "Rebel and I have been talking, and we think that this club needs to move into more legitimate businesses." They all looked around at each other, trying to figure out where Hawk was going with that. I waited. "With that being said, we need to diffuse this animosity with the Satans. It's gone on long enough and we have spent years watching our backs because of them. I am sick and tired of it, and I know you all are, too." He paused for a brief moment, then continued, "They want a piece of the action, so why don't we give it to them? I'm prepared to give them the gun and drug business. We'd keep a small percentage of their profits, but they would get the majority of it. It's what they have always wanted, and I think this will broker a peace between the two clubs." He waited again for what he was saying to sink in, then continued, "Ok, let's open this up for discussion."

That was my cue to get the discussion rolling. "As Hawk said, he and I have discussed this. And I will be honest with you all—I was skeptical at first. I mean, we would be taking a pay cut. But after I thought about it, I like it. Think about not having to worry about the ATF or the Satans. Think about making money from other, honest and legitimate possibilities." I waited for a second and then added, "Think about a porn studio or an escort service. I'm sure you all are down with that. Right?" I let that sit and waited.

"So what kinda cut we talking about?" Doc asked.

"Right now, you all split twenty percent of the gun and drug money. I have not ironed out all the details yet, but if this deal happens, I'm guessing your cut will drop down to five percent. I know that sounds like a lot, but if we add money from porn and escorts, then your income will double and your families will be safe. That's a promise."

"Fifteen percent, that is a lot," Ryder added. He thought for a moment. "But if we get the other businesses up and running quickly, I guess it won't be quite as noticeable. How long before we get the other options in full swing?" he asked.

Hawk replied, "Well, I'm looking at about six months. I've been looking into these options for a long time now and have already made some contacts. We'd need to find locations for the escorts—something nice, not a dump or a studio. I don't think we will have any problems finding talent. I mean, we've got a gold mine right here at Kandi's."

"So, when do you plan to make the tradeoff with the Satans?" Ryder asked.

"Well, if you all agree, Rebel and I will set up a meet. Ryder, we'd like you there as well. Obviously, there would have to be a transitional period, but they will probably start getting their full cut in three months. So you all are only looking at losing your fifteen percent over a three-month period."

"Man Hawk, I know that three months doesn't seem like a long time, but shit, I've got an ex-wife and two kids that expect their money every month. What am I supposed to do during those three months? Spike asked.

"Yeah, I've got bills to pay too. Where am I supposed to get the income the guns gave me during those three months?" Doc added.

"I know you all have legitimate concerns. And, I know you all have bills to pay. But think about how much better off we will be in the long run. Yes, you will lose money. No, it won't be forever. And when all is said and done, you will end up making a hell of a lot more once our legitimate businesses are up and running. Everyone loves porn and pussy, guys. We can't lose going down that road," Hawk replied.

"I don't know, man. Something about this is just not sitting right with me. Let's put the money issue aside for a minute and think about what we are doing. I mean seriously, you are asking us to go to bed with the Satans. When have we ever been able to have peace with those fuckers, let alone go into business with them?" Spike said.

Hawk was silent for a moment, and then said. "I want you boys to think about why you joined the MC. Some of you came to us for the money, some for the brotherhood, and others because you were just plain Harley enthusiasts. But, did you join to do illegal shit? Did you join to constantly worry about getting caught by the authorities? Did you join to have your families in constant jeopardy? Some of you crazy fuckers will say yes to all those questions, but I know for a fact that the majority of you will say no. It's not the life that you signed up for, but it's the life you have been dealt. What we are offering you is a chance to change it. A chance to keep your families safe and your ass out of jail."

They were powerful words and I could tell that they were actually contemplating what Hawk just said. He waited again, and then added, "Look, I know you all need to think about this. If you don't have any more questions, let's take a break for now and meet back here at 6 pm to vote. Sound good?"

They all nodded in agreement and the meeting broke up. I waited until the guys left the meeting room, then asked Hawk, "So what do you think?"

"I understand their concerns, but I think they will see it our way. I guess we will know at 6 pm. Come on. I don't know about you, but I need a drink."

"Hell yeah, I'm down for that." I followed him to the bar.

After we got our drinks, I decided to check in with the girls. I had left Tiny with them and I was sure he would have called if something was wrong, but you can never be too careful.

Ari answered the phone on the second ring. "Hey, Fire!" Part of me wished she wouldn't call me that, but the other part of me kind of liked it that she had a pet name for me. I just wished she would've come up with a better one.

"Hey, doll. You girls doing ok? Tiny treating you right?" I asked.

"We sure are. But he's not as fun to have around as you are," she said teasingly.

"Well, I sure as hell hope not, for his sake. And for yours too. You're mine!"

"Geez, you don't have to be so possessive. I know who I belong to. I've always belonged to you. Speaking of which—when you gonna make this official? I'm sick of waiting." My dick suddenly got hard. *Fuck her, she knows why I'm waiting.*

"Oh, just you wait, sweetheart. I'm gonna have you begging for it, and once you get a taste, you will want it all the time." She didn't respond. I waited patiently for her to say something, but all I heard was silence. I started getting pissed and began yelling into the phone.

"Rebel, stop yelling. Ari is fine," I heard on the phone. It was Emma's voice.

"What's going on?" I asked frantically. All I could think of was that something had happened to Ari.

"Everything is fine," Emma said into the phone. "Ari just had a panic attack or something. I'm not sure, but she was having trouble breathing. Everything is fine now. Here, let me put her back on the phone," Emma replied.

"Hey, Rebel," Ari said sweetly into the phone.

"Baby, are you ok?" I asked, relieved to hear her voice.

"Yes, baby, I'm fine," she replied.

"What happened?" I asked.

"I ... I don't know, Fire. I just thought about what you said and it just worried me a little."

"Worried you? Why?" I asked curiously.

"Because I ... well, I never ... I mean, well, you know ..." she said shyly.

Oh, shit. I never thought about that. "Baby, I'm sorry if I scared you. I didn't mean to scare you. I want to be with you more than anything, but I'll do whatever you need, babe. If you need to take things slow, we can do that. If you need gentle, I can be gentle. Whatever it takes, however long it takes. You are my girl, baby, and I won't do anything to hurt you. If I seemed like I was rushing things, I'm sorry. I've been in love with you for a long time, darl'n, and I can't help but look forward to the time when we can finally be together." I felt so bad that I had scared her. I hoped she understood what I was saying. I waited patiently for her to respond.

"I know, Fire, I know. I want to be with you, I really do. Please don't think that I don't, or even that I am afraid of you. I just don't want to rush things. Is that ok?"

"That, my dear, is more than ok." I paused for a moment then added, "I gotta run, babe. I should be back at the house in a couple of hours. I love you."

"I love you too, Fire," she said and hung up the phone.

Fuck, I wasn't expecting to have that conversation with her already, but I guess it had been bothering her. Hopefully I have put her mind at ease.

An hour or so later, the boys started filtering back to the meeting room. I was really curious how this vote was going to go. Frankly, I was not sure it was going to go the way Ice wanted it to. Hawk and I were the last two to enter the meeting room. Hawk sat at the head of the table and said, "Well, we all know why we are here. I'm not going to discuss the tradeoff anymore, unless you all have any lingering questions." He looked around the room to see if anyone had anything to say, but it appeared that all were ready to vote. Hawk continued, "All those in favor of trading the gun and drug business off to the Satans, say aye." He then added, "Aye," and then looked at me.

"Aye," I replied. I then looked at Doc, who was sitting next to me.

"Aye," he said, looking at Ryder. We went around the room, all brothers agreeing to the tradeoff until we got to Spike. He was a nay. We continued around the room and by the time we were back around the table to Hawk, we had ten in favor of the tradeoff. The vote was not unanimous, but majority ruled and we were going to move forward with the plan. Ice had been right. But hell, wasn't he always?

Hawk slammed down the gavel. "It's done. We'll get to work on the next steps. Meeting adjourned," he said as he started to get up.

"Hawk, before we adjourn, I wanted to ask—what about appointing a new VP?" Ryder asked.

Oh shit, I hadn't thought about that. I watched Hawk eagerly to see how he was going to handle that one.

"You are right, Ryder, we need a new VP. But I've had so much going on right now, I haven't really thought that much about it. Why don't you all get your recommendations together for our next church, and we can go from there? Sound good?" Everyone nodded in agreement. "Are we done?" All were in agreement and they started to get up and leave the meeting room.

As the boys left the room I looked over at Hawk curiously. After they were all gone, I said, "Well, what next?"

"Call Ice, let him know that the club voted and he is free to negotiate with the Satans. I'll call Gypsy and set up that meeting. Once I get the meeting set, I'll let you know so you can tell Ice. Oh, and you might want to fill Ryder in before that meet to let him know that Ice is alive as well."

"Got it. Do you need me for anything else?" I asked.

"Nope, go home to the girls. Tell Honey I'm coming for dinner." He smiled.

"I sure will, Hawk. See ya later."

Club business was done for the day. It was time to head to Ice's house and spend some time with my girl. I headed out and when I got to my bike, I decided to send Ice a text.

> Club voted the tradeoff. It's a go. We'll be in touch with a meeting time.

He replied,

> Good work. I'll wait to hear from you.

I got on my bike and headed back to the house. When I got back, I walked into the house to find Tiny and the girls all sitting at the table, playing cards. They were all laughing and having a good time, and I found myself a little jealous. I wanted to be the one to make Ari laugh. But shit had to get done for my club, and for now, the club had to come first. Ari was used to the life and I knew she would understand.

"Hey, Rebel! Come join us. We are just getting ready to deal a new hand," Ari said.

I was dog-tired and really didn't feel like playing cards. I said, "I'm really beat, sweetie. Can I take a rain check?" I asked. Without waiting for a response, I turned to Honey and asked, "Anything left for dinner?" I was starving and needed food.

"Sure, Rebel. Everything is in the oven so it will stay warm. I think Hawk is on his way over, too."

I thought, *Of course he is. He never misses an opportunity for a free meal, especially if Honey is cooking.*

"Thanks, darl'n." I walked into the kitchen, got a plate, and started going through the food. The oven contained pot roast, mixed veggies, and mashed potatoes; this was one of my favorite meals.

Just as I was sitting down to eat, Hawk walked in. Before he could say anything I said, "Food is in the oven. It's still warm."

"Fuck yeah," he said. He said hello to the girls and told Tiny that the truck was outside for him to take back when he was ready. After he got his plate, he sat down next to me.

"Meeting is set for Monday at 10 am with the Satans," Hawk said quietly, so that only I could hear. "Make sure you let Ice know."

"Got it." I pulled out my phone and texted Ice. His reply was exactly what I'd expected.

Well done. I'll be there.

Hawk and I finished dinner, then hung around and chatted with the girls for a bit. Then I remembered that I needed to talk to Ryder about Ice. I stepped outside and called him. He answered on the second ring.

"Hey, Reb, what's up?"

"Hey man, I need to talk to you. Can you meet me at Betty's in about a half hour?" I asked.

"Sure thing. Is something wrong?" he asked.

"No, I just have some good news to share with you."

"Ok, see you in a few." We hung up and I went back inside.

"Hey everyone, I need to step out for a few minutes. I should be back in about an hour," I said to the group.

Hawk looked at me curiously. I said, "I'm meeting Ryder at Betty's." Hawk nodded, but now the girls were looking at me curiously. They didn't need to know everything. I grabbed my keys and headed out the door.

When I got to Betty's, Ryder was already there. He was sitting at a booth in the back looking worried. I smirked; I was about to make his day. As I approached his booth I said, "Hey, man. I've got some big news to tell you."

"Oh yeah?" he responded.

"Let's go upstairs. This needs to stay private for now," I said. He dropped some cash on the table and we headed up the back stairs.

When we got into the meeting room Hawk had set up for the club, I told Ryder to take a seat. Fucker still looked worried and I loved making him feel that way. *Maybe I should let him stew for a bit. Fuck, naw. I can't do that to my brother.*

"Ice is alive." I really didn't know how else to say it except to just blurt it out. The look on his face was priceless and I couldn't help but chuckle.

"What. The. Fuck!" he responded. "What's going on, Rebel?"

I spent the next thirty minutes explaining to him everything that had transpired over the last several months. Needless to say, he left Betty's a happy man. It's a disconcerting thing in the MC world to lose your leader. The brothers feel lost and out of sorts. There is always another to take his place, but losing a leader like Ice is harder than most because the majority of the club believes he's irreplaceable.

CHAPTER 20

Caden

I was impressed that Hawk and Rebel convinced the club to agree to the tradeoff, and at how quickly they'd scheduled the meet. I hadn't thought that the club would agree so quickly; I assumed they'd delay their vote to think on it more. But once they'd agreed to the tradeoff, it looked like I'd be able to return the land of the living in just a few days. I was grateful for that—I missed my girl, and was aching to get home to her and start our life together.

On Monday morning, I got up early to prepare for my meeting with the Satans. The meeting could make or break our club, and my entire future rested on its outcome. I went over every detail in my head until I was confident that I had all my talking points outlined.

I got to Jimmy's about an hour early. I needed to stay hidden from our guests; I didn't want to be discovered as soon as they walked into the warehouse. I wanted to be prepared in case they were going to react first and think later. I wasn't about to let that happen, so I waited in the shadows. After about forty-five minutes, Hawk, Rebel, and Ryder walked in.

I walked out from one of the back rooms and Ryder's face lit up with a huge smile. "Fucking A, it's sure good to see you alive and well, boss." He walked over to me and shook my hand and pulled me into a hug—one of those manly hugs where you kinda half-hug and pat each other on the back. It was good to see him. Just then, we heard the side door open. I quickly turned and went back into hiding.

I watched from the crack in the door as Gypsy and Skid walked in. They all shook hands, and Hawk said, "Thank you both for agreeing to this meet."

Gypsy replied, "How could we not? You said that it would be worth our time. You and I both know that the only thing worth our time is if you boys are giving us what we have always wanted. And I know you know what that is."

Gypsy wasn't a bad guy, for the most part. He did bad shit, shit that I really didn't approve of, but he had a good head on his shoulders and usually thought first and acted later. Skid, on the other hand, was the exact opposite. He was very reactive and was my biggest worry.

"I think we are on the same page, Gypsy," Hawk said. "But before we get into the details of this meeting, there is something that you need to know." He hesitated and looked over to the room I was hiding in. That was my cue. Slowly, I opened the door and walked out. Gypsy and Skid just looked at me in shock.

"Do my eyes deceive me, or is that a dead man walking toward us?" Gypsy asked, sounding calmer than I'd expected.

I walked up to the group and shook Gypsy and Skid's hands. "Last I checked, I was very much alive. This meeting is to ensure that it stays that way. You boys ok with that?" They looked at each other and both nodded. "Good. Why don't we have a seat?" We all sat down at the table that was situated in the center of the room.

"Before we get involved in discussions, I think you need to tell us why you wanted the world to think you were dead," Skid said.

I figured it was best not to beat around the bush, so I said, "I killed Mark Grayson." I let that hang in the air between us and waited for some kind of reaction. What I got was totally unexpected.

"Grayson is dead?" Gypsy asked.

"Yeah, dead and buried," I replied. Then I said cautiously, "If you have a problem with that, then we need to deal with that first."

"Fuck yeah, I have a problem with that." Skid said. He started to get up out of his seat and I assumed he was going to come at me next, but Gypsy grabbed his arm and glared at him. A silent conversation took place between the two of them. Gypsy's face reminded me of the look my dad used to give me when he was displeased with me, but didn't want to embarrass himself. Which, frankly, was all the time so I knew that look well. Anyway, after a few seconds, Skid returned to his seat with a grunt.

"Before I react to this, tell me, Ice—why did you kill Grayson?" Gypsy said.

It was a question I hadn't expected, but I realized that I needed to be honest with him. "Grayson kidnapped my old lady. He stripped her naked and tied her to a bed and planned to rape her, but then changed his mind. The fucker made me watch." I hesitated briefly.

"What else?" Gypsy asked. I could tell that Gypsy knew I was not telling him everything. I'd known him for a long time, and he didn't get to be Club President by not being observant and smart.

"What else?" I replied. "Isn't that enough?"

"It could be, but it's not. Is there more to this that you are not telling me?" Gypsy said.

Fucker. He either knows about my connection to Grayson, or the son of a bitch is fucking with me. Now is not the time to play his games. "Grayson was my brother. We shared the same father and there were issues between us that needed to be resolved. Only one of us was going to come out of that basement alive and I made damn sure it was me."

"Thank fuck!" Gypsy said. "That fucker has caused my club more problems than he was ever worth. I knew about the connection between the two of you. He'd been after you for a long time. I just wasn't sure if you did. You just confirmed that."

Surprised by his reaction, I said, "So, you are glad he's dead?" I was still expecting blowback at any minute.

"Hell yeah, I am. The only reason we backed him was because he kept us out of jail on numerous occasions. But, I swear he had some serious psychotic issues. Take that whole situation with Brianne and your old lady. He was fucked in the head, I'll tell you that. We agreed to keep Brianne for him, but that was as far as our arrangement went. When he started talking about taking your club down, that's when I backed off and left him to his own devices. I had basically washed my hands of him before he went missing. His absence made my club life a hell of a lot easier," Gypsy replied.

Well, shit. This whole charade was totally unnecessary. "Is Brianne still alive?" I asked.

"Yes, but she is so hooked on crank it isn't funny," Skid said.

Fucker! He's the one that got her hooked in the first place. Out loud I said, "Ok, well, I totally read this situation all wrong. I played dead 'cause I thought the Satans would retaliate on my club and me for killing Grayson. Apparently I was wrong. I didn't realize I was doing you all a favor. Needless to say, when I had the chance, I went batshit crazy on him and now he is dead. I'm not sorry, and I gather by what you are saying, you aren't sorry either."

"Hell no! I'm relieved."

"I'm not," Skid said angrily. He looked right at me and yelled, "That fucker killed my friend!"

Gypsy turned back toward Skid and said, "If you can't keep your opinions to yourself then there's the door," as he pointed toward the door.

Gypsy turned back toward me and said, "As I am sure you have experienced in leading your own club, sometimes you have to deal with insubordination in the ranks. My apologies." He waited for a minute to ensure that Skid had heeded his words, then added, "So, I have the feeling you are about to make my day and give my club what we have always wanted from the Knights. So what's it gonna be, Ice?"

That had been a lot easier than I'd expected. I had a feeling that I was going to have to deal with Skid down the road, but I'd cross that bridge when I came to it. For now, it was time to move forward with the difficult part of this conversation. "Before I go into the details of why we wanted this meeting, I need you to know that none of this goes through unless you agree to all my terms."

"Your terms?" Skid asked. Gypsy glared at him again and he immediately checked himself.

"Yes. First, the deal I'm about to offer you only happens if you release Brianne to me. We will get her help and take responsibility for her." Gypsy looked over to Skid, who seemed a little reluctant.

That asshole doesn't want to give up his plaything. But with his president silently telling him to agree, he eventually nodded his head in agreement.

I continued, "And second, the war between our clubs stops now. We have been feuding for many years now, and frankly, I want it to stop. I have not remained President because I waste my time fucking around with vendettas. They get us nowhere, and the end result is us choking each other out. It's bad for business, our clubs, and our families. I want us to find a peace. I want my club to go back to being motorcycle enthusiasts." I chuckled at the thought.

"And how do you propose to make that happen?" Gypsy asked.

"Well, first, I want to keep the Knights and the Satans moving forward. We both know what has to be done, and the last thing we want is to hurt business. If we do that, nobody wins. I know deep down we are all smarter than a loaded gun." They nodded again and I continued, "With all that being said, why don't you confirm for me what is it that the Satans want from us?"

Gypsy hesitated for a minute, looked at Skid, and then said, "We want your gun trade."

"That's what I thought. So, this is what I propose. We hand off the gun trade to the Satans, with the Knights receiving five percent." I shrugged. "Consider it a finder's fee for passing that business to the Satans. As I move my club into more legitimate enterprises, that percentage has the potential to disappear." I waited. I'd learned that it's always best not to talk too much, especially when you are trying to sell something.

They thought for several minutes and then Gypsy asked, "Ok, say we agree. Do we have full reign over that operation, or will the Knights be breathing down our backs all the time about the way we do things?"

It was a good question. "You have full reign. As long as we get our five percent, consider the Knights a silent partner," I replied.

"Ok, and how long before that five percent disappears?" Gypsy asked.

"I don't have anything definite yet, but I'm hoping it will be less than a year."

"Why now?" Gypsy asked. We've been feuding over that gun trade for years."

"I want my club out of guns," I replied.

"So just like that, you give us the gun trade that you have held onto for dear life for years? Something is not adding up, Ice."

"I understand your skepticism. I'd be the same way. The only thing I can do to convince you that I am totally on board with this is to explain further. I'm tired of the drama and bullshit. I'm done with guns and so is my club. I want our families to feel safe, and I don't want any heat from the ATF. With all that being said, you can be damn sure that I will bust my ass to make sure this moves as quickly as possible," I replied.

"You sound sincere, but I don't know, man. Your offer sounds too sweet to be true. Surely you can understand that."

"I know, I get it. But I can assure you there are no hidden agendas here. Gypsy, you have known me for a long time. We may have always been on opposite sides in the past, but you know I'm an upfront guy and I don't play fucking games."

"Yeah, you are a man of your word, that much is true." He paused for a moment, then added, "Look, I'll tell you what. You know I can't make any kind of decision on my own. Let me bring it to our table and see what my boys think. You good with that?"

"Absolutely. And I am safe to return to the land of the living?" I asked, confidently.

"Yeah, man. Like I said before, I'm glad that cocksucker is dead. You should have made contact with us right away, you could have avoided a lot of trouble on your end."

"I'm sorry about that. I assumed the worst and went with it. My mistake. I was so focused on ensuring that my old lady and family were safe, I didn't think about talking to you first."

They got up to leave. Gypsy said, "Ice, Hawk, Ryder, thank you for the sit-down. I think we have made a lot of progress here. This has been a long time coming, and I am glad that we are finally seeing eye-to-eye on things. I will call church tonight and we will vote on this. Hopefully, I'll have an answer for you in the morning. How do I reach you?"

I gave him my cell number, shook his hand, and thanked him for listening to what we had to say. I felt euphoric. We were finally moving this club in the right direction and I couldn't have been more pleased.

After Gypsy and Skid left, Hawk asked, "So, what do you think, Ice?"

"It went better than I expected. Don't ya think?"

He replied, "I do. Definitely better than I expected."

"Boys, we made history today. This is a good thing. Now, you know what I want to do?" They laughed and I continued, "I want to get my bike and my cut and get my ass home to my girl and my family. We can inform the rest of the club about my resurrection in the morning. You boys good with that?"

"Hell yeah!" Rebel replied. "Do you need help?"

"Naw, I'm just gonna leave the cage at the storage place. We can get a couple of prospects to get it later."

"You keeping the cage?" Rebel asked.

"Yeah. Ari doesn't have a car. Until I can get her a nice one, she can drive that one," I replied.

"Oh, she's gonna hate you for that. You know your sister wants a Harley," Rebel said.

"She's not getting a damn Harley from me. Her old man can buy her one!" I laughed. Rebel knew I was talking about him and suddenly a look of guilt came across his face. "What?"

"Well, I've been meaning to talk to you about that," Rebel said sheepishly.

Hawk jumped in and said, "Ryder, I think this is our cue to leave. Catch you boys back at the house later. Honey is cooking again tonight, and you know I'm down for that. Ryder, you should join us."

"Thanks, Hawk. You know I never miss an opportunity to eat," Ryder said.

After Hawk and Ryder left, I turned to Rebel and said, "So, you been meaning to talk to me?"

He looked down at the floor for a moment and then looked me dead in the eye. "I know you already know this, but I am in love with your sister." He waited for my reaction and when he didn't get anything, he continued, "Well, the other night, I told her, and she loves me too. I want her to be my old lady, Ice, but I need your blessing. If you don't approve then I will leave her alone."

"Rebel, man, you're one of my closest friends and my brother. I love you as if you were my blood. I couldn't imagine anyone better for my sister or anyone who would make a better brother-in-law. You've always had my blessing," I replied.

"Really?" he asked, surprised.

"Really." I paused for a moment and then added, "But remember what I told you: you break her heart, and I will personally make your worst nightmares come true. And then I'll kill you."

He smiled. "I know. I've seen your wrath. You can be damn sure I won't be breaking her heart, ever. I swear. I'm still in awe of the fact that she feels the same about me."

What a pussy. But, as I have learned recently, love will turn even the toughest bastard into the biggest pussy. I'm proof of that.

Rebel continued, "Thanks, Ice. I'll see you back at your house. I'm glad you're coming home!"

"Me too! Now get outta here! I got shit to do!" I laughed and we headed out of the warehouse.

CHAPTER 21

Emma

Things had been pretty quiet around the house since Caden's memorial service. I hadn't heard a word from him since he had been here several weeks ago. Every day I prayed that he was ok and that he would return to us soon. I knew that Rebel or Hawk would tell me if something had happened to him, but it still didn't deter me from worrying about him.

Being cooped up in the house all the time was making me crazy. I knew it was for our own good, but enough was enough. It's a good thing that Ari, Honey, and I all got along so well, or the situation could have been much worse.

We worked really hard to find things to occupy our time. We'd played board games. We'd spent time in the kitchen experimenting with new recipes. Honey even tried to teach Ari to cook, but that didn't go so well. We'd had a blast the other night playing cards with Tiny. He never really spoke much in the times I had spent with him in the past, but it seemed like he was starting to feel a little more relaxed around me. He was a really funny guy and had us girls in stitches. Other than Tiny, we'd only seen Hawk and Rebel. Apparently the rest of the club still thought Ice was dead. I was looking forward to when this charade would be over with and we could go on with our lives.

I was sitting in the living room, reading and actually enjoying the quiet, when the front door opened and in walked Hawk, followed by another member of the club. I recognized Hawk's companion, but couldn't remember his name.

Hawk said, "Hey Emma, do you remember Ryder?"

Yes, now I do. Ryder. I need to remember that.

"Yes, of course. Hi, Ryder. Nice to see you again." I looked over at Hawk curiously. I'd thought that we were keeping the club away from the house until Ice could return. He caught my concern and smiled, but he didn't say anything to answer my silent question. If I didn't know better, I'd have thought that he was up to something.

"Where are the girls?" Hawk asked.

"Ari is taking a nap and Honey is down in the basement getting something out of the freezer for dinner tonight. She should be up any minute."

"Oh, okay," he replied, sounding a little disappointed. What was up with that? Was he disappointed that Honey would be back any minute, or was he disappointed that she wasn't here to greet him?

The boys went into the kitchen and got themselves something to drink. I didn't pay attention to what they were drinking, as I had found that those guys would drink alcoholic beverages at any time of the day. It was strange to me, as I'd grown up with the notion that alcohol shouldn't be consumed before 6 pm. I didn't know why, exactly—it was just what my parents always said. I returned back to my chair and my reading.

Hawk and Ryder plopped themselves down at the bar and started to talked about some meeting they had that day and that they were pleased with the outcome. Obviously, they didn't mention any details. Heaven forbid they talk about club business in front of an old lady ... but I strained to hear anyway, hoping to hear a clue about something.

Honey came up a few minutes later and I thought she actually blushed when she saw Hawk sitting at the bar. Those two definitely had something going on, I would have bet money on it. "Hey guys," she said. When Hawk saw her, his eyes lit up. He smiled and said hi back while Ryder got up and gave her a big hug.

"Hey, Honey girl! I've missed you!" Ryder said as he squeezed her tight.

"I've missed you too, big guy!" she said, smiling. Hawk watched Honey and Ryder closely. I think if he could have, he would have literally turned green. I had to laugh to myself. These big, bad bikers—they talked the big talk and walked the walk, but deep down they were a bunch of sensitive guys looking for the same thing we all are looking for: love. For some silly reason, that thought made me smile.

Just then, I heard a bike pull up. *That must be Rebel,* I thought to myself. While Honey chatted with Hawk and Ryder, I walked over to the window to confirm my suspicions. As I watched out the window, I realized I knew that body like I knew the back of my hand. The rider got off his bike, removed his helmet, and looked directly at me watching from the window with a smile. Caden was home!

"Hey guys, Ice is home!" I squealed. I ran to the door and literally jumped into his arms as he walked through the threshold. He held onto me so tightly that for a minute I believed his strength would crush me. But I knew better. The man that I loved so dearly wouldn't do anything to hurt or harm me. He had proven that over and over again.

Hawk and Ryder sat calmly at the bar watching our display of affection while Honey strolled over to give Caden a hug. When he finally released me, after giving me a kiss, he turned to Honey and said, "Hey, sweetheart." She walked into his arms and he gave her a hug. Then he said, "I told you I'd be back."

"Yes, you did! But I have to say, even though we knew you were alive, I found it hard to believe until I actually saw you!" Honey replied. Then she took her right hand and hit him hard on the arm. "Don't you ever scare me like that again!" she scolded.

She still loves him, I thought to myself. *Maybe I was wrong about her and Hawk?*

"Yes, ma'am," Caden replied. "Is dinner ready yet? I'm starved," he said. Suddenly, I felt like an intruder.

"Not yet, but I'll get working on it right away." Honey replied and went back to the kitchen to work her magic.

Everyone was talking and chatting with Caden and I stood back and watched his family welcome him home. Ari came out of the bedroom, still sleepy, and said, "What is going on out here? You guys make more noise than the sex-crazed women at a Maroon 5 concert!" When her eyes focused, she realized why there was so much commotion going on. "Caden! You're home!" she yelled, and she practically knocked him over as she ran into his arms.

"Hey, doll face! How's my best girl?" I knew that I had nothing to be jealous of—I mean really, she was his kid sister. But after the display with Honey and now this, I just felt like I didn't belong. *Will I ever feel like I am part of the family?*

Suddenly, I started to feel sick. Whatever Honey had started cooking made my stomach turn and I felt like I was going to vomit. I immediately ran upstairs. The last thing I needed was to get sick in front of everyone.

I made it to the bathroom in the nick of time and my stomach released everything that I had eaten earlier. As I hung my head over the commode, I felt a hand gently grab onto my hair and hold it back. I glanced up and saw it was Caden.

"You ok, baby?" he asked.

Grabbing some toilet paper to wipe my mouth, I replied, "Go away. I don't want you to see me like this."

He laughed. *Why is he laughing at a time like this? I'm so embarrassed.*

He said, "Baby, we are in this for the long haul. I'm gonna see you at all times, even ones like this. It's gonna be all the way, baby, for better or worse. So, please tell me, are you ok?"

When I was confident that my stomach had settled, I got up and walked over to the sink. I needed to brush my teeth and get that nasty taste out of my mouth. All the while, Caden just stood there watching me. When I was done, I turned toward him and said, "I'm fine. I just suddenly felt ill, but I feel better now."

"Are you sure?"

Reassuringly, I replied, "Yeah, I'm sure. I don't know what came over me." *Well, actually I do. Damn green-eyed monster ... but he doesn't need to know that.*

We both went back downstairs and everyone asked if I was ok. I assured them all that I was just fine, but Honey looked at me curiously as if she knew something that I didn't.

Not long after, Rebel returned and everyone started the chatter again, with Caden being the center of attention. I knew they were glad to have him back, but I wanted him all to myself. I knew I was being selfish, but that didn't matter. He was mine.

Honey finished cooking dinner and everyone got up to get a plate. My stomach was still feeling a little queasy and I thought it best that I didn't eat. I pulled Caden aside and said, "I'm still not feeling 100 percent. I think I'm gonna go lay down for a bit."

He looked worried and asked, "Are you sure you're ok?"

I gave him a hug and a kiss on the cheek. "Baby, I'm fine. Just don't feel much like eating, and getting sick has made me really tired. You don't mind, do you?"

"No, babe. You get some rest. I'll be up later," he said.

I smiled, made my excuses, and went upstairs. I hoped I would feel better after I took a good long nap.

CHAPTER 22

Caden

I woke up the next morning to the sound of Emma getting sick again in the bathroom. *I don't care how fine she says she is, she is going to the doctor.* I got up and walked into the bathroom. "Babe? Did you get sick again?"

"Yeah," she said sadly. "I've been up most of the night. I must have caught a bug or something. I feel awful."

I walked over to her and scooped her up into my arms. "You are spending the day in bed. If you are not better by tomorrow morning, you are getting your ass to the doctor. Understood?" I'd just gotten my life back, and everything was falling into place—this was not the time for her to be sick.

"Ok," she agreed reluctantly. I could see that she was really tired and weak. I went over and lifted her up and carried her to the bed. Her body felt limp in my arms. I was beginning to worry.

I placed her back on the bed, covered her up, kissed her on the cheek, and told her to get some rest. I proceeded into the bathroom to shower.

When I came out of the shower, Emma was sound asleep. I dressed as quietly as I could. The last thing I wanted to do was disturb her now that she was finally sleeping. After I dressed I walked downstairs. Honey and Rebel were in the kitchen having coffee.

"How's Emma feeling?" Honey asked.

I shook my head. "Not so good. I expect her to stay in bed most of the day. I told her if she isn't better tomorrow, she's going to the doctor."

"I'll make a batch of chicken soup. Maybe that will help settle her stomach," Honey said and went back to drinking her coffee.

"Thanks, dear. Keep an eye on her for me, will ya?" I asked and then turned toward Rebel. "We need to head out soon."

"What for?" he asked.

"'Cause we have shit to do," I said.

"Like what?"

What the fuck? Did these boys go all soft on me the weeks I was away?

"First of all, we need to call church. We need to get moving on the new clubhouse and move forward with the gun trade. Is that ok with you?" I asked sarcastically.

"Hey man, I didn't mean ..."

I cut him off. "Then don't fucking ask 'like what?' when I say we have shit to do!" Man, you could tell that I had been away for several weeks.

"Yes, sir!" Rebel replied. That was more like it.

Just then, my phone rang. I pulled my phone out of my pocket and checked the caller ID. It was Hawk. I said, "Hey man, I was just about to call you."

"Great minds, boss. By the way, did I tell you how good it is to have you back?" I laughed. Hawk had never wanted to be President, but he'd done a great job in my absence. He continued, "So, I figured you would want to call church today. Got any specific time in mind? I'll let the boys know."

I looked at my watch: 9:30 am. I thought for a moment and then replied, "Let's do 11."

"You got it! See you at Kandi's," Hawk replied, and then he hung up the phone.

"Hawk?" Rebel asked.

"Yeah," I replied.

"What'd he want?"

"He wanted to know what time to call church. I told him to set it for 11." I paused briefly then added, "See, that's called being proactive. You could learn something from him."

"Ice, man, I'm sorry. I'm not sure what I did to piss you off this morning, but please, cut me some slack. You've been gone for weeks. Nothing has been the same since you left and all the guys, including myself, need to readjust. I'm not trying to be a dick here, I'm just saying, cut us some slack."

He was probably right. I said, "Ok, I hear ya. I'm just ready to get shit back to normal now that I am back. I went weeks without my cut, and now that I have it back, I want my club back too. Surely you can understand that."

"I do, really, but you have to understand where we are coming from, too," he replied. As much as I hated to admit it, he was right. I needed to remember that when I was reunited with the rest of the club.

After my conversation with Rebel, we still had some time to spare, so I went back upstairs to check on Emma. She was still passed out. I decided it was best not to bother the poor thing; she needed the rest. Instead, I went back downstairs and grabbed another cup of coffee.

When I came back downstairs, Honey asked, "Ice, would you like some breakfast?"

I smiled. She was always taking care of her boys. "Naw, darlin', I'm good."

She looked a bit disappointed, but said ok and went about rustling around in the kitchen. I assumed she was getting started on Emma's soup.

When we arrived at Kandi's, Rebel dismounted his bike and hesitated for a moment. I turned back to him and said, "What now?"

"Well, it is probably not a good idea for you to just waltz in there, don't ya think?" he said.

"Why the fuck not?" I asked.

"Maybe because they all think you're dead?"

Oh fuck, I didn't think about that. I'd been too busy worrying about getting back on track, and that minor detail had just escaped my mind.

I nodded. "Yeah, man, you're right." I thought for a moment, and then added, "Maybe you should go in first and give everyone the heads-up."

"I don't think that is a good idea, either. Shouldn't it come from Hawk?"

Fuck, he's right again. I looked around the parking lot. It appeared that everyone was already there. Most of them probably slept at Kandi's since they didn't have a clubhouse to sleep in anymore.

I texted Hawk:

> Hey, I'm outside. Do the boys know I'm alive?

He texted back:

> Come on in, brother. They are all waiting for you.

Now that was what I wanted to hear. I looked to Rebel and said, "It's all good. They know."

"Fucking A!" he said. "Then let's go, boss!"

We walked into the club and immediately my fellow brothers welcomed me back to the land of the living with numerous embraces. Many were asking questions as to what had happened and why I'd been playing dead. But all in all, they were happy to see me—not that I'd expected anything less.

"Thank you all so much! I sure as hell missed you guys!" I said graciously. Then I added, "Are we ready for church?"

"Hell, yeah!" and "Yes, sir!" I heard in a jumble of voices.

We all headed into the back meeting room and started the meeting. I explained to them why I'd done what I did and how I saw the club moving forward, and we talked about plans for the new clubhouse. We also discussed plans for our new porn and escort business. The boys were pumped—I should have known that the mention of pussy would motivate them. Doc recapped the club's finances, and I had to admit, I was surprised to hear how well we were doing. Our legitimate businesses were really paying off, and once we added our newest venture into the mix, the club would be a lucrative business entity. All in all, it was a productive meeting. Everything was going exactly how I had hoped. I couldn't have been more pleased.

After the meeting, we hung around Kandi's for a couple of hours. The boys wanted to have a celebratory drink in my honor. Fuck, it was good to be back.

When all the camaraderie had concluded, we did have more business to tend to. Hawk and I headed out to the warehouse he had procured for our new clubhouse. He was excited to show me what he'd found. He didn't know that I had already seen it, but I wasn't going to burst his bubble. I was proud of him.

When we got there, he started explaining to me his ideas on how he wanted to refit the space. His ideas were fucking awesome—when we were done it was going to make a kick-ass clubhouse.

"So I was thinking that we could put the bar here, with the kitchen next to it through that archway," Hawk said, gesturing to an area not far from the entrance. "And over here, this could be the lounge area. We could get a flat screen TV for that wall." He pointed to a huge wall that would be perfect for a large TV. He took me through a doorway to another big room. "I thought this could be our chapel. A lot more space than we had before, don't ya think?" he said.

"This place is fucking awesome, Hawk! You did real good." I paused for a moment and then said, "What about sleeping quarters?"

"Ice, man, that's the best part. Wait until you see the upstairs. There is enough space for five more rooms than what we had before." He led me up the stairs in the back of the building and I saw that he was right. The space was huge!

"What about the grounds?" I asked. I had seen that the parking lot was adequate. We would have to fence in the area, but we'd expected that. He led me over to one of the windows that looked out the back of the building and I could see it was perfect. There was enough land to accommodate the grilling and barbeque pit, picnic tables, and even space to include a small play area for the kids.

"Hey, give Mareck a call. He'll cut us a deal on the construction." Mareck Construction was a local construction company just on the outskirts of Erie. We'd helped Jason Mareck a while back when he needed some muscle to fend off some people after him for his gambling debts. We didn't clear his debts, but we made them an offer they couldn't refuse by them allowing him ample time to repay his debts. It was a win-win, and now he owed us a favor.

"Shit, Ice, I didn't even think of Jason. I'll call him as soon as we get back."

"Hawk, you did a great job finding this place. The boys are going to love it. You picked a perfect location, too—not too far outside of town. Once we get done making it our own, it's going to fucking rock!" I paused for a brief moment and then added, "Ya know, I can be a real dick about most shit. I've been so wrapped up in getting back to the club and Emma, I never thanked you for all that you have done. I couldn't ask for a better VP!"

"Awwww, shucks, Ice," he said in a very thick southern drawl. He shuffled his feet and added with a laugh, "Should we hug or something?"

"Fuck you! See if I ever say anything nice to you again!"

"And the dick is back," he said, patting me on the back.

I laughed. "Come on, fuckface. Let's get back. It's almost dinner time and I'm hungry."

"Honey cooking tonight?" he asked shyly. That fucker had had a thing for that girl for as long as I could remember, but he'd never had the balls to tell her. Then when she and I hooked up, I guess he realized he'd lost his chance. But now, things are a little different. I had Emma, so there was no reason for him not to stake his claim.

"Why do you ask?" I asked teasingly. When he didn't answer, I continued, "Wanna join us for dinner?" I knew that was what he was waiting for. I knew that in my absence, he'd come and gone to my house as he pleased. But now that I was back, the fucker had manners. I laughed. "And while we are on the subject of Honey, why don't you tap that already and claim her as your old lady?"

"What the fuck you talking about?" he said defensively.

"If I have to explain it to you, old man, then you don't deserve her," I said, laughing all the way out the building and to my bike, Hawk following closely behind me. He didn't say a word, just mounted his bike and started it up. He'd gotten the message loud and clear.

CHAPTER 23

Emma

I woke up feeling like a truck hit me. I could smell something cooking downstairs and although the smell wasn't repulsive, the thought of eating anything made me feel sick. Whatever the hell bug I had, I wished it would just leave already. I looked over at the clock on the nightstand: 5:30 pm. *What the hell? Have I slept the entire day away?* I had to get up. I was sure Honey needed some help. Caden and Rebel were going to be back soon.

I brushed my teeth, washed my face, and threw my hair into a ponytail. I got dressed in a pair of leggings and a big, oversized shirt and headed downstairs. As I'd suspected, Honey was in the kitchen, busy cooking up something. She looked up when she saw me. "Well, there is our little sleepyhead. How are you feeling, hun?" she said.

"A little better. Have I been sleeping all day?" I asked, confused.

"You have. Whatever bug you got, it has totally wiped you out. I made you some chicken soup. Are ya hungry?" she asked.

"I'm sorry, Honey, but I don't think I can eat anything right now. But I would love some ginger ale, if we have some."

"We don't, darlin', but let me shoot a text to Ice to pick some up for you. The boys are on their way back. He texted a few minutes ago to let me know that Hawk would be joining us for dinner." She pulled out her phone and sent the text.

Why did he text her to say he was on his way home and not me? Oh, for fuck's sake, Emma, stop it. He didn't text you because he probably knew you would be sleeping, I told myself. I had to get control over the green-eyed monster growing within me. It wasn't like me to be like that. But lately, my emotions had been everywhere. It felt like my period was about to start any day now. *My period?* I thought for a moment. I couldn't remember the last time I'd had my period. Well, it was no wonder with all the stress I'd had to endure over the last several weeks. I shrugged. I was sure that's all it was. Stress.

"Can I help you with anything?" I asked Honey.

"No way, baby doll, you are not well. You just sit your pretty little self down and relax. I got this," Honey replied. "And just so you know, Ice gave me strict orders: if you are not better by tomorrow, you are going to the doctor."

"Yeah, he told me," I said, defeated. I hated doctors. It was just a little bug. But I had learned that when Ice said he wanted something done, it got done. Plain and simple.

A little over an hour later, the boys returned. Rebel returned first, then Caden and Hawk returned not long after.

Caden approached me when he arrived. "Hey beautiful, how are you feeling?" he asked.

"I'm doing better," I replied.

"You look awful," he said.

Gee, thanks, tell me what you really think. I just wanted to run upstairs and cry. Not only did I feel like shit, apparently I looked like shit too.

He could see my reaction to his comment and followed up with, "No babe, I didn't mean it like that. You just look like you still don't feel well. That's all."

"I know. I guess I'm just a little overly sensitive these days. Once I feel better it will pass," I replied.

He went into the kitchen and got a glass out of the cupboard. He filled it with ice, grabbed the bottle of ginger ale from the bag he was carrying, and poured it into the glass. "Here ya go, darlin'. Hopefully this will make you feel better," he said as he handed me the glass.

"Thank you." I felt like a child. *Why is he treating me this way? Why is he being so distant?* He sat down next to me on the couch and pulled me into him. Ok, so maybe he wasn't being distant. Maybe I was reading into things that aren't there. *Shit, I should just go back to bed.*

He leaned over and whispered sternly in my ear, "You are going to the doctor tomorrow."

"Yes, Dad!" I replied sarcastically. The look he gave me could have sawed through wood, but I didn't care. He was not my father, nor my keeper. I had a mind of my own, damn it. But I knew that wouldn't change anything. I would be seeing a doctor tomorrow; he wouldn't have it any other way.

Everyone sat down to dinner and Caden motioned for me to sit next to him. I was starting to feel nauseated again and really didn't want to eat anything, but Honey poured me a bowl of soup and encouraged me to sit down to eat as well. Reluctantly, I agreed.

"Do we happen to have any saltines?" I asked.

"We sure do," Honey replied. She rummaged through one of the cabinets and produced a box of crackers. Hopefully between the crackers and the ginger in my soda, my stomach would start to feel better.

Like a good little girl, I ate my soup. It was really delicious, and the combination of the soup and the crackers was making me feel better. Maybe that was all I needed. Maybe I wouldn't have to go to the doctor tomorrow. I was still feeling fatigued, but I was sure that was just from throwing up so much.

After dinner, we all hung around the house talking. Ari and Rebel went for a walk together and about two hours after dinner, Hawk reluctantly left. We all headed to bed not long after. As Caden and I were getting ready for bed, I asked him, "Caden, why do you treat me like a child?"

He looked at me curiously. "Babe, I don't treat you like a child."

"Well, actually, you do. I'm a grown woman and I have been taking care of myself for a very long time now. I think I can determine if I need to see a doctor or not."

He stopped walking toward the bathroom and turned toward me. "Babe, you may think of it as me treating you like a child. And I can understand why you might think that. But let me explain something to you. You have been and always will be the love of my life. I have loved you long before I even knew I loved you, if that makes any sense. When we were kids, you always looked up to me and I felt that it was my role to protect you. Now that we are adults and have found our way into each other's hearts, the last thing I want is to see you hurt or sick. I worry. I've waited so long for you and I refuse to lose you now."

"Wait a minute, who said anything about you losing me? I'm in this for the long haul. I thought we have already established that."

"That's not what I meant. If something is wrong and you are really sick, I want you to get it fixed. I don't want you sick. I want you healthy and happy and by my side, always." He paused for a moment and when I didn't say anything, he continued, "So you may think I am treating you like a child, but babe, it's only out of concern for your health. That's all."

"Oh," I said, realizing that I had been ridiculous to think that way. And when I thought about it, I realized that if the tables were turned, I would feel the same way. I just wasn't used to being with someone that I cared that much about, or who cared so much for me. He was right. "Well, if you put it that way, I guess it's ok," I replied teasingly.

He laughed, walked over to me, and kissed me deeply. If he hadn't been holding on to me, my legs would have given out just from that kiss. I looked up at him. He was so tall; his 6'5" build towered over my 5"8" height. His size was mesmerizing and made me feel so protected. He said, "So, are you calling the doctor tomorrow?" He still hadn't shaved his beard, and it made him look damn sexy. I found myself hoping he decided to leave it.

"Yes, I will," I replied. His mere size was intimidating enough, not to mention the incredible hold he had over me. Suddenly, I no longer felt sick. All I wanted to do was to devour him.

My arms slid up around his neck and I started to play with his hair. It was soft and silky in my hands and I realized that I'd never paid attention to the fact that he had absolutely gorgeous hair. It was slightly longer in the back, his curls grazing his neck. "So, big boy," I said teasingly, "if I promise to go and see a doctor tomorrow, can I get something in return?"

"Oh babe, you know I will give you anything I have to give. All you have to do is ask," he replied eagerly. He knew exactly where I was going, and to my liking, he was playing along.

"Can I have you?" I asked seductively. "Now," I added with more urgency.

He stood there for a moment, looking at me intently. Then a wicked smile came across his face. He took a step back, held out his arms, and said, "Baby, I'm all yours."

That was all I needed to hear. I fell into his arms and it felt as if I was coming home. All my worries and fears of the last couple of days vanished. I was exactly where I needed to be and he was all mine.

Caden wrapped his arms around me and buried his face in my neck. His warmth seeped into my skin and his strong arms surrounded me. The chemistry between us was so strong it filled the entire room. It pushed through my body with a fierceness that I couldn't control.

He leaned down and kissed me, softly at first, and his kiss gradually became more urgent. My legs went weak as his tongue tangled with mine. The intensity of his kiss left me breathless and wanting more. I reached for the edges of his shirt and started to lift it up. I needed to feel the heat of his body against mine. Hell, I needed to feel him. All of him. He released my lips and took a step back. Suddenly, I felt cold and alone. I asked, "What's wrong?"

I could see the love in his eyes. I could also see lust. He wanted me just as much as I wanted him. So what was the problem?

He said, "Nothing is wrong. I just want to make sure you're feeling up to this. The way I'm feeling right now, I may not be gentle, babe. I just want to be sure that you are feeling better."

The last thing on my mind at the moment was how I was feeling. But he was sweet to worry about me. About half an hour ago I'd felt like shit, but now I was on fire. I felt amazing. I nodded, and then added with confidence, "I have never felt better."

He growled at me and pulled me to him, claiming my lips again. I thought, *I could kiss this man for eternity and never tire of him.* The slow, demanding way he took my mouth to his made me cling to him like a starved kitten clawing for food.

I dropped down onto my knees and started to fumble with the fly of his jeans impatiently. I wanted his cock badly. He helped me by sliding his jeans down just far enough for me to get to the prize. He looked so damn sexy standing there with his pants partially down his legs.

Once his cock was free, I took it in both hands, gently running my hands up and down his shaft as I looked up at him. I licked the little notch on the underside of the head, moving my tongue rapidly against him.

"Baby!" he growled, letting me know how good I was making him feel. He reached down and tangled his fingers in my hair, urging me to go on. He didn't have to coax me too much as I gladly wrapped my mouth around his cock. I opened my mouth, sucking him in as deep as I could, taking his tip to the back of my throat. Every bit I could take I worked with my tongue over and over. He moaned in pleasure. My left hand rested on his balls, alternately rolling and gripping them. His cock got harder in my mouth and he started moving his hips toward me a little with each stroke. He grasped at my hair a little tighter. Looking up at him, I could see his eyes were fixated on the pleasure I was providing him. The expression on his face was one of pure need. In that moment, I realized that I held a power over him like no other. This powerful, strong man who provided guidance and protection to everyone around him was at my mercy. The feeling was intoxicating.

Before I knew it, I was being lifted from under my arms. In one fell swoop I was turned around and bent over the bed. Caden had undone my jeans and they hovered at my knees as his cock entered me from behind. Holy fuck, it felt good. He growled again when he was completely sheathed by me and pumped me hard. He was so deep inside me I thought my insides would explode. He maintained a hard, steady rhythm and before I knew it I detonated into one of the most amazing orgasms I had ever had. Caden came right after me, grunting and groaning as he released himself inside me.

Afterwards, we snuggled as we were lying in bed. It seemed that neither of us was tired, but neither of us had anything to say. As my thoughts wandered, I realized that Caden had never told me why Mark did the things he did. Lying here in the quiet seemed like the perfect opportunity to ask. "Cade? Can I ask you something?"

"Sure, babe," he replied.

"Why did Mark target you and the club? Was it because of me?" I asked guiltily. I worried that I had brought everything down on the club by going to him for help. And if that was the case, I needed to make amends somehow.

"No, Emma, it wasn't your fault. It was mine," he replied.

"Yours?" I asked indignantly. *Why would it be Cade's fault? That's ridiculous.*

He was quiet for a while and then he spoke. "Yes, sweetheart, it was my fault. I really wanted to wait to tell you everything, but since you asked, I realize that it is not fair to keep you in the dark. Mark did all of this because of me. He found out about our relationship when we were kids and used you as a pawn to destroy me and my club."

"But why?" I asked. None of this made any sense to me. Why would Mark go after Caden and the club? Had he even known Caden?

"That's the tricky part. You see, Mark Grayson was my older half-brother." I stared at him in shock, unable to say anything. Caden took advantage of my silence to continue. "You remember me telling you about Ace and how he took me under his wing? He treated me as if I was his own kid. My rise through the club was not only because of my merits, but also because of his influence."

"Yeah, I do. You told me that he was like a father to you," I replied.

"Well, he is my father."

"What?" I asked, confused.

"I believe it's true. From what Mark told me, Ace gave him up for adoption. His mom didn't want him and Ace didn't want his kid involved with the club. I gather he did it to protect him from the chaos that we live in. So the Graysons adopted him. My mom knew Ace from high school. I don't know much about their relationship, but apparently Mom and Ace hooked up later, and I was the result."

"So why did your mom marry Tyler and not Ace?" I asked.

"I guess he did the same thing to her that he did to Mark's mom. He didn't want this life for his son. My meeting him after Mom and Tyler's deaths was by chance. At that point, I was a grown man and he really didn't have much say in my life. I assume that he felt sorry for me and wanted to do what he could to help."

"Did you know? Did you know that he was your dad?"

"No, he never said a word to me about it, but he did treat me as if I was his son."

"So, Mark knew about you?"

"Yes, and apparently he had been planning this whole charade for quite some time. He told me that I took what should have been his. He wanted the club life and he wanted Ace."

"How did he know you were Ace's son?" I asked.

"I don't know. He said he just knew. I never really gave him time to explain. However, one of the last things he said to me before he died was that I stole his life. That thought obviously fueled how he felt and what he did."

"Oh God, that's so sad." I stopped talking and took in everything Caden had just told me. It was so hard to believe that Brianne and me getting taken and Caden killing his own brother all resulted because a man was jealous. Because a man wanted a different life than the life that he had been dealt. It made me think about all the horrible things that happen to people every day for the same reason. It was just so sad that people could be driven to such drastic extremes by jealousy.

"Caden? Are you ok with all of this?" I was worried for him. It was a lot of baggage for him to deal with, not to mention that he would have to face the fact that he murdered his own brother. *Can a man survive that kind of guilt?* I asked myself. Only time would tell.

He squeezed me tighter to him and said, "Babe, I'm not the kind of guy to get consumed by guilt. I've told you before that I've killed many. I'm not proud of it, but if I were in those situations again they would all result in the same outcome. I did what I had to do."

CHAPTER 24

Caden

Finally, everything is going my way. Today we meet with the Satans and finalize the details of the tradeoff. Today, if all goes as planned, Brianne will be safe. Today, I will make my formal proposal to the most amazing woman I know. Today, she will say yes.

After I left the house I headed straight to Kandi's to meet up with Hawk and Rebel. The meeting with the Satans was at 10 am and I wanted to go over a few things with the boys before we met up with the Satans at the Waterford Hotel.

I was in the back office at Kandi's when Hawk and Rebel walked in. "Hey, Ice. Are we ready for this?" Hawk asked.

"I sure as hell am," I replied. "This is a big day in Knights history. Do you boys feel it?" I asked. They both looked at me as if I'd lost my mind. I continued, "We are moving out of guns, boys! This is huge!"

"Oh yeah, that," Rebel said. I got the impression that he wasn't fully behind this move.

"You have a problem with this, Reb?" I asked.

"Naw, man. I'm good with it," he replied.

"So what in the hell is your problem?" I didn't understand his indifference and it was pissing me off. I didn't want a fucking cheerleader. Hell, I'd never get that from Reb anyway. But shit, I wanted some enthusiasm.

"Shit, Ice. I'm sorry, man. I'm all in, I really am. I just got a lot of other shit on my mind today."

"Well, get your head on, brother. We have a big deal going down today and I don't want anything to go south. You got me?"

"Yes, sir."

I then added, "And if this shit has anything to do with my sister, I don't want to hear about it." I'd given him my consent to date Ari, and I'd been glad to see her so happy for the last couple of days. But I was not about to become a relationship counselor for them. Their relationship was their business and I wanted no part of it.

"I hear ya," he replied.

"We need to be in Waterford in about an hour. I wanted us to meet here a little early 'cause there are a couple of things I want to go over before we do this." They both nodded in agreement. "If everything that Gypsy and I agreed upon the other day goes according to plan, they will have Brianne with them. I'm not sure what kind of condition she will be in, but I want you to get her to a hospital as soon as the meet is over. If everything that we have learned is true, she is going to need to detox. Hell, we will probably have to send her to rehab, too."

"Do you think they are still drugging her after all this time?" Hawk asked.

"I do. At this point, she is hooked. They may not be drugging her to keep her quiet anymore, but now they are drugging her to feed her addiction." I waited and then added, "I wouldn't be surprised if she has been sexually abused, too—especially by Skid. That guy is an animal when it comes to women."

"That poor girl," Hawk said, shaking his head. I nodded silently. I didn't know Brianne personally, but I sure as hell knew that whatever shape we found her in was going to break Emma's heart. I didn't want Emma to see her right away, which is why I hadn't said anything to her about the possibility of getting Brianne back today. Once she'd been in the hospital for a couple of days and was getting on the mend, I would take Emma to see her.

"Anything clse?" Rebel asked.

I thought for a moment and then shook my head. "Nope, I think we are all good here. Let's go get this shit done."

We left Kandi's and went straight to the hotel. We had about ten minutes to spare, so we grabbed a table and ordered a beer.

A few minutes later, Gypsy and Skid walked in with a tall, thin brunette in tow. Brianne. *Fuck, what did they do to her?* She had two black eyes, looked like she hadn't eaten in weeks, and was as high as a kite. Skid seated Brianne at another table and told her to stay. She didn't say a word, just nodded. They came over to our table and sat down.

"Is that Brianne?" I asked Gypsy. He nodded. "What the fuck did you do to her?" I asked.

"Look, Ice, you didn't specify what condition she needed to be returned to you in, just that she needed to be alive. I told Skid to go easy on her, but obviously my VP has a different idea on what the term easy means." He glanced over to Skid, clearly not happy with him. It was equally clear that Skid couldn't care less that his president was pissed at him. If he were my VP, I would have beaten the shit out of him. Thank God my brothers weren't like that.

We ironed out all the details of the tradeoff, bearing in mind all that we had agreed upon before. When we were done, Gypsy got up from the table. "Ice, it's been a pleasure doing business with you. I guess, for now, this makes us partners with the Knights." He turned to Skid and said, "Say your goodbyes to Brianne. You won't be seeing her again."

Skid replied, "Fuck that shit, she was just a temporary plaything anyway. I don't need to say anything to her."

What a fucking asshole. One of these days, I'm going to meet up with him in a dark alley and only one of us will walk away. I really hated that guy.

Gypsy replied, "Very well then. Let's go." They turned to leave and walked out of the bar. Brianne didn't even notice their departure. She just sat at her table, staring off into space.

I walked over to her, knelt down beside her, and said, "Brianne, my name is Ice. I am a good friend of Emma's." She didn't say a word. She just gave me a blank stare. This was not going to be easy. I asked, "Brianne? Do you understand what I am saying to you?" Still nothing.

I turned to Rebel and said, "Take her to the hospital. I don't think she will give you any problems. She is so fucking out of it, I don't think she has a clue what is happening around her."

"You got it, boss," Rebel replied. He walked over to her and reached for her hand. She gave it willingly and they walked out of the bar together.

"What the fuck, Ice!" Hawk said. "Do you think she can even be fixed?"

"Hell, Hawk, I have no fucking idea. But for now, not a word to Emma. I don't want her to know that we have Brianne. I don't want Emma to see her like this. Let's get her to a hospital and see what a doc has to say first." Hawk nodded in agreement.

CHAPTER 25

Emma

Well, like a good little girl, I'd gone to the doctor. The news was shocking—no, it was fabulous. Or was it? Caden was going to freak out. My head was spinning from the news and I could not think straight. One minute I was happy and the next, I was terrified. How in the hell was I going to explain this to him?

I was upstairs getting some laundry together when Caden got home. I could hear him talking to Honey and Ari downstairs and I wanted to go down and greet him too, but I was scared. If he saw me, he would see it all over my face and I wouldn't get the opportunity to tell him in private. I needed to wait. I needed to stay where I was and wait for him to come to me.

Just then, I could hear him coming up the steps. *Oh, shit. How in the hell am I going to tell him?* He walked into the bedroom as I turned away from him toward the closest.

"Hey, babe. What'cha doing up here?" he asked.

Not looking at him, I replied, "Just getting some laundry together. Do you need to have anything washed?" I asked.

"Everything I need washed is in the hamper, babe. I can do the laundry if you want."

Still not making eye contact with him I replied, "I got it, but thanks."

"Emma?"

"Yeah?" I replied, still not looking at him.

"Emma? What's wrong, babe?"

"Nothing," I said.

"Emma, you have not looked at me since I walked into this room. What's going on?" he asked. I could hear the worry in his voice, but I just didn't know how to tell him. He then added, "What did the doctor say?"

"She said I should get a dog," I replied, finally looking up at him as the tears started to well up in my eyes. I walked over to the bed and sat down. I tried so hard to hold back the tears, but I just couldn't. I was a raging mess of emotions and I had no control over any of them.

He looked worried ... or maybe just confused. "A dog?" he asked.

Pulling myself together, I replied, "Yeah, a dog. A great big one, I think."

He walked over to me and sat next to me on the bed. He grabbed my hand and said, "Let me make sure I've got this right. You went to the doctor today because you have been sick now for three days, right?"

"Yes."

"Ok, I'm with you on that. Now, perhaps we can clarify the next part. The doctor didn't say what was wrong with you, she just said that should get a dog, and not just any dog, a big one. Right?"

"Yeah, that about sums it up."

He sat there for a couple of minutes just letting it all sink in and then he said, "And what is the dog supposed to do for you? Well, besides giving you a pet, I guess."

"The dog isn't for me. It's for the little one."

"The little one?" he asked.

"Yeah, the little one. I was worried about having the little one grow up in your world and she suggested that we get a dog. It seems like the perfect solution and I think we should get one right away." I knew I was being vague, but I was just having such a hard time saying the words. Shit, I was having a hard time believing it myself.

"Emma, babe, I'm sorry. But you've lost me, sweetie. Do you think you could be less cryptic and fill me in on what's going on?"

"Ok, you are right. Just answer me this. Can we get a dog?"

"Yes, baby, whatever you want. Now what is this all about?"

"I'm pregnant." There. It was said, and it dropped to the floor like a lead weight. Cade was quiet, so quiet that he was scaring me. I looked up to make sure he was ok and there were tears in his eyes. Relief washed over me. He wanted this child. He wanted me. That was all I needed to know.

Finally he spoke. "Really? Are you really pregnant? Are you really going to have my kid?" he asked.

The tears were flowing freely now and I nodded. Caden scooped me up in his arms and swung me around. He was so happy. Suddenly, he stopped spinning and put me down. "Oh, babe, I'm so sorry. Are you ok? I didn't hurt you or the baby, did I?"

I laughed. "No, Cade, I've never felt better. Your son and I are fine."

"Son? Is it a boy?" he asked encouragingly.

Silly man, like I could really know this early. "I don't know what it is, but it feels like a boy," I replied. I then added, "Would you be ok if it ended up being a girl?"

"Oh baby, it doesn't matter to me if it's a girl or a boy. All I care about is that you and our child are healthy. You are amazing and I love you so very much."

He hugged me again and when he released me I asked, "So can we start looking for a good rescue?"

"What?"

"A rescue, you know, so we can get our dog."

He laughed. "Yeah, baby, we can. Let's go downstairs and share our good news."

I grabbed his arm. "No! Wait. I don't want to tell anyone yet. I'm only six weeks along. Can we wait a little longer, please?"

"Oh. I didn't think about that. I guess we can," he replied. I could tell he was disappointed. I thought to myself, *would a couple of weeks really make a difference?*

"You know what, let's tell everyone."

He looked at me with so much excitement in his eyes, "Really Emma, are you sure?" He asked, hopeful.

I smiled. His reaction to the news warmed my heart so much, that at that moment, I would have agreed to anything. "Yes, baby, we can share our news." I paused for a moment and then added, "Oh, and one more thing."

"Whatever you want, babe."

"Are you gonna make an honest woman of me?" I asked as I held up my naked left hand.

"You bet, baby—as long as you are ready for the ride of your life."

I smiled and walked over to him. "I've never been more ready for anything in my entire life."

CHAPTER 26

Caden

Holy fuck! I'm gonna be a dad. I was still trying to wrap my head around Emma's news. Don't get me wrong, I was thrilled, but I was also scared as fuck!

Emma and I went downstairs. Ari and Honey were in the kitchen preparing dinner and Rebel was on the phone. Not paying much attention to him at first, Emma and I shared our news with the girls.

"OMG!" Ari squealed. "I'm gonna be an aunt!" She ran over to Emma and hugged her tightly then stepped back. "Are you really pregnant?" She asked as if she just couldn't wrap her head around it.

Emma laughed, "Yes, Ari, I'm really pregnant and yes, you are gonna be an aunt."

She ran over to me and jumped up and down. I really had not expected such excitement from my kid sister, but it was really touching to see her this way. "My big brother is gonna be a daddy! I'm so excited!" she sang to some odd melody that I swear she just made up in her head.

Honey gave Emma a hug to congratulate her and I swear I could see a tear in her eye. I hoped that she was happy for us. She and Emma had been getting along really well from what I could see. Then I remembered the abortion she'd had not long after she came to us. I hadn't thought about that ... I should have been more considerate of her feelings. For a brief moment I felt like an ass, but then I saw her smiling and realized that her tears were most likely mixed feelings. She walked over to me and said awkwardly, "You're gonna make one hell of a dad, Ice."

"Ya think?" I asked, trying to lighten the conversation a bit.

"Hell yeah, I sure do," she said confidently. Her confidence made me smile.

"Thanks, Honey, that means a lot." I waited until the awkwardness of our conversation subsided a bit, then added, "Well, this could not have come at a better time. We are all whole, we've finally made peace with the Satans, and things should be calming down now significantly."

Before anything else was said, we heard Rebel yell, "What the fuck! What do you mean you don't know where they are?" I quickly turned toward him and watched him curiously. He was pacing frantically in the living room. I had no idea who he was talking to, but he was obviously agitated.

"Find them! I'll get there as soon as I can!" He hit end on his conversation and looked at me with total despair in his eyes. "Ice, man, I need you. We have to go to Belfast."

– THE END –

Stay tuned for the next installment in the Knights of Silence MC series, Celtic Dragon.

ICE ON FIRE PLAYLIST

Skid Row – *In A Darkened Room*
Foreigner – *Cold as Ice*
Bon Jovi – *Blaze of Glory*
Bon Jovi – *Prayer '94*
Bon Jovi – *Always*
Bon Jovi – *Roller Coaster*
Needtobreathe – *Brother*
AlterBridge – *Wonderful Life*
Aerosmith – *Don't Wanna Miss A Thing*
Lynyrd Skynyrd – *A Simple Man*
Goo Goo Dolls – *So Alive*
Molly Hatchet – *Flirtin with Disaster*
Rainbow – *Stone Cold*
Gregg Allman – *I'm No Angel*
AC/DC – *Highway to Hell*
Neil Young – *My My Hey Hey*
Lonestar – *I'm Already There*
Pat Benatar – *Fire and Ice*
AlterBridge – *Breathe Again*

ACKNOWLEDGEMENTS

First of all, I would like to thank my friends and family. Without their support, I never would've had the courage and the vision to bring to life Caden and Emma's story.

I would like to thank my husband Kevin. You've never doubted me or my abilities. All that I am - you let me be. I would be totally lost without your comments, ideas, suggestions and edits. And, I promise you, I will write that pirate book. I would like to thank the residents of the towns of Waterford and Edinboro, Pennsylvania. Your hospitality while I was visiting and doing my research went above and beyond what I ever expected.

Also, I'd like to thank Hannah Hall. Your comments and suggestions during all the writing stages of this book truly helped shape the outcome. It makes my writing so much easier to have someone to share my thoughts and ideas.

I would also like to thank Alicia Freeman and Michelle Cates. Your PR abilities are amazing and I couldn't ask for two better personal assistants. You ladies are a pleasure to work with and I could not be more grateful for all that you do for me.

And finally, I would like to thank Ellie and Carl Augsburger of Creative Digital Studios for their insightful ideas, creative cover designs, marketing materials, promotional trailer and comprehensive editing. I am blessed to have such a talented creative design and editing team. You both are top notch!

ABOUT THE AUTHOR

Amy Cecil writes contemporary and historical romance. Her novel, ICE on FIRE is the second book in the Knights of Silence MC series. When she isn't writing, she is spending time with her husband, friends and various pets.

She is a member of the Romance Writers of America (RWA) and the Published Authors Network (PAN). She was a winner in the 2015 and 2016 NanNoWriMo writing contests and a nominee in Metamorph Publishing's Indie Book 2016 contest in historical romance. ICE was voted the "Baddest MC Novel" in the Brain to Books CyCon in April 2017. ICE was also nominated in the OUAB17 awards for Sizzling Romance of the Year and Gripping Standalone Novel.

She lives in North Carolina with her husband, Kevin, and their three dogs, Hobbes, Koda and Karma and her horse, Baylee.

Knights of Silence Series

This is Amy's fourth novel. And don't fret, she is already working on Book 3 in the Knights of Silence MC Series, *Celtic Dragon*. In the meantime, she wants to hear from you!

Amazon: https://www.amazon.com/Amy-Cecil
Goodreads: https://www.goodreads.com/authoramycecil
Webpage: acecil65.wix.com/amycecil
Facebook: www.facebook.com/authoramycecil

DON'T FORGET...

If you've read *ICE* and loved it, then please leave a review.

Authors love reading reviews!

----

[i] Poem by Hannah Hall

[ii] Poem by Hannah Hall

[iii] Poem by Hannah Hall

Made in United States
Orlando, FL
03 March 2023

30649954R00102